Streets of Redemption

Evan Blake

Published by Evan Blake, 2024.

Streets of Redemption

By: Evan Blake

This is a work of fiction. Names, characters, places, and incidents are products of the author's imagination or are used fictitiously. Any resemblance to actual persons, living or dead, events, or locales is purely coincidental.

Cover Design by Michael Thompson
Edited by Michael Thompson

Disclaimer: This book contains mature themes, including violence, language, and depictions of life in challenging urban environments. Reader discretion is advised.

The streets never let go, and neither does the fight for freedom....

Introduction

Life in the heart of the city could either break you or mold you into something tougher than the streets themselves. For **Jamal Taylor**, survival wasn't a choice—it was all he'd ever known. Raised by a single mother lost to drugs and a system that never seemed to care, Jamal learned early that dreams didn't always come true. The streets of **Eastwood**, a notorious neighborhood in the city, demanded a kind of loyalty that would swallow you whole if you weren't careful.

By the age of fifteen, Jamal was already running errands for **Big D**, the neighborhood's most feared drug lord. But at twenty-two, he was starting to feel the weight of the life he had inherited. Jamal had spent years watching friends disappear into the prison system or the graveyard. Now, as he faced a crossroad between continuing down the same path or stepping into the unknown, the streets whispered to him, daring him to find a way out.

What happens when the desire for redemption clashes with the pull of the only life you've ever known? For Jamal, the answer would come at a price far greater than he ever imagined.

Chapter 1: Trapped in the Game

The late afternoon sun blazed over Eastwood, casting long shadows on the cracked pavement. Jamal Taylor wiped the sweat from his brow as he stood outside **Donny's Barbershop**, waiting for his next run. He could hear the usual sounds of the block—cars screeching down the street, music blaring from half-broken speakers, and the low hum of people hustling. It was the life he'd known since he was a kid, but lately, it felt like a prison.

"Yo, Jamal," called **Rico**, his longtime friend and fellow runner. "Big D wants you at the spot in an hour. Something big going down."

Jamal nodded, barely looking up. He knew what that meant. Another drop. Another risk. Every time he made a delivery, he felt like he was one step closer to either getting locked up or gunned down.

And after last night's news—**Trey** had been shot over on 7th Street—Jamal's mind had been racing. Trey was like a brother to him, but now, just like that, he was gone.

As he leaned against the brick wall of the barbershop, he spotted his younger sister, **Keisha**, coming down the block. She looked just as tired as he felt, her school uniform wrinkled and her backpack slung low over her shoulder.

"Jamal!" Keisha shouted, her face breaking into a smile as she hurried over.

He smiled back, but his eyes were weary. "What you doin' out here?"

Keisha shrugged. "Had to get out the house. Mama's trippin' again. Didn't wanna be around when she got started."

Jamal's heart sank. Their mother had been strung out for years, her addiction tightening its grip with every passing day. He had stepped into the role of caretaker for Keisha when he was barely old enough to care for himself. At sixteen, Keisha had already seen too much of what the streets had to offer, and Jamal feared that no matter how hard he tried, she'd end up lost to them, just like so many others.

"You stay outta trouble, aight?" Jamal said, ruffling her hair. "Go on home, I'll be back later."

She rolled her eyes, but a small smile tugged at her lips. "Yeah, yeah. You too."

Jamal watched her walk away, his chest tight with guilt. She deserved better than this. He did too. But how could he break free when the streets held him so tight? Every time he thought about leaving the game, something pulled him back—whether it was loyalty to Big D or the need to put food on the table. His construction job applications hadn't gone anywhere, and he knew deep down that guys like him didn't get second chances.

The hour passed quicker than he'd hoped, and soon enough, Jamal found himself walking toward **The Spot**, a dingy corner store that served as Big D's front. As he entered, the air inside was thick with tension. **Big D** sat behind the counter, a massive man with tattoos running down both arms, his eyes cold and calculating.

"Jamal," Big D said in a low voice. "I need you to take care of somethin'. Big order. Ain't no room for mistakes this time."

Jamal's stomach twisted, but he kept his face straight. "What's the move?"

Big D leaned in, his voice dropping even lower. "We got some new product comin' in, and you're gonna be the one makin' the run. **Ghost** and his boys been sniffin' around my turf. This needs to go smooth, ya feel me?"

Jamal nodded, though his mind raced. Ghost. The name alone sent a chill down his spine. Ghost wasn't just another hustler—he was a predator, someone who thrived on chaos. If Ghost was lurking around, this was about to get a lot more dangerous.

"Don't worry, I got you," Jamal said, even though doubt gnawed at him.

Big D's eyes narrowed as he studied Jamal. "You best. 'Cause if you mess this up, you ain't got no more chances, understand?"

Jamal swallowed hard and gave a stiff nod. "I got it, D."

As he walked out of The Spot, Jamal's mind was racing. The weight of the streets pressed down on him, heavier than ever. He knew the game was rigged, and no matter how hard he tried, the streets always pulled you back. But with Trey gone, Keisha on the edge, and Tasha slowly becoming the only bright spot in his life, Jamal had to decide whether he would be trapped forever—or if he'd find a way out, even if it cost him everything.

The sun had set now, casting the streets of Eastwood in shadow. As Jamal made his way toward the drop-off, the reality of his situation hit him like a brick. This wasn't just another run. This was a turning point.

And the streets? They were watching.

End of Chapter 1

Chapter 2: Ghosts in the Shadows

The night crept in, casting long, dark fingers across the streets of Eastwood. The familiar sounds of the neighborhood had shifted—no longer the chaotic hum of day-to-day hustle, but something darker, more sinister. Jamal could feel it in his bones as he made his way through the maze of alleyways. The streets weren't just dangerous—they were alive, watching, waiting for him to make the wrong move.

He tightened the straps on his backpack, where the package from Big D sat heavy against his back. Normally, a job like this wouldn't make him nervous, but tonight was different. Trey's death had rattled him, and the mention of **Ghost** had sent his mind spinning. Ghost was more than a rival—he was a force of nature, a predator who fed on fear and chaos. The thought of running into Ghost or one of his crew made Jamal's stomach churn. He needed to get this over with. Fast.

The rendezvous spot was a crumbling warehouse on the far side of town, just past the tracks where the city's light faded into the murky shadows of forgotten streets. Jamal had been there before—too many times. It was a dead zone, perfect for drops, with no one around to witness anything that might go down.

As he neared the warehouse, Jamal's thoughts wandered back to his sister, Keisha. He couldn't get the image of her out of his head—the way her eyes had been tired, her smile forced. She was slipping. He'd tried his best to keep her away from the streets, but in Eastwood, it was like trying to hold back the tide. Sooner or later, it pulled you under.

She deserved better. They both did.

Jamal approached the warehouse cautiously, scanning the area for any signs of trouble. The lot was empty, save for a few broken-down cars and the flickering glow of a streetlight that had seen better days. His heart pounded as he slowed his steps, his senses on high alert.

He reached into his jacket, feeling the cool metal of the piece he kept tucked there. Just in case.

The warehouse loomed ahead, its rusted doors half-open, like a gaping mouth waiting to swallow him whole. Jamal swallowed hard and made his way inside.

The interior was dark, save for a few slivers of moonlight cutting through the cracks in the ceiling. The smell of damp concrete and mildew filled the air. He heard the faint drip of water somewhere in the distance, but otherwise, it was dead quiet.

Too quiet.

Jamal's grip on his gun tightened as he walked deeper into the shadows. **Ray**, one of Big D's top lieutenants, was supposed to meet him here. But there was no sign of Ray. No sign of anyone. "Ray?" Jamal called out, his voice echoing through the empty space. He waited, the silence pressing down on him. Something wasn't right.

His nerves buzzed with tension. He'd been doing this long enough to know when something was off. And this—this was wrong. Every instinct screamed at him to turn around and get the hell out, but he couldn't. Not with the package on his back and Big D waiting for the job to be done.

Suddenly, a figure stepped out of the shadows, and Jamal's heart jumped into his throat. It wasn't Ray.

It was **Ghost**.

The man stood tall, his presence commanding the darkness around him. Ghost was a name that suited him—his skin was pale, almost ghostly in the dim light, and his eyes were dead, as if there was nothing human left behind them. He wore a black leather jacket, his hands in his pockets, his expression cold and calculating.

"Look who we got here," Ghost said, his voice low and menacing. "Little Jamal. Thought you'd be smart enough to stay outta my way."

Jamal's pulse quickened, but he forced himself to stay calm. He'd heard about Ghost, seen what he was capable of, but this was the first time he'd ever come face to face with him.

"Didn't know this was your spot, Ghost," Jamal said, trying to keep his voice steady. "I'm just doin' a drop for D. Nothin' more."

Ghost's lips curled into a smile, but it didn't reach his eyes. "That right? You think you can just walk through my territory without payin' your respects?"

Jamal's mind raced. He needed to get out of this, but Ghost wasn't the kind of man you could reason with. He thrived on violence, and right now, Jamal was nothing more than prey.

"I'm just tryin' to handle my business," Jamal said, taking a small step back. "I don't want no trouble."

Ghost's smile faded, and his eyes narrowed. "Trouble's already here, kid."

Before Jamal could react, two more figures emerged from the darkness behind Ghost. His heart sank. He recognized them—**Spade** and **Rico**. Rico wasn't supposed to be here, and the look in his eyes told Jamal everything he needed to know.

Rico had betrayed him.

"Rico," Jamal said, his voice low, filled with disbelief. "You set me up?"

Rico looked away, guilt flickering in his eyes for a brief moment before hardening. "Had to, J. Big D's time is up. Ghost is takin' over. You either roll with us, or you get rolled over."

Jamal's mind raced, anger and betrayal surging through him. Rico had been his boy since they were kids. They'd been through hell together. And now this?

"I ain't rollin' with nobody," Jamal said, his hand tightening around the grip of his gun. "I'm done with this shit."

Ghost chuckled darkly. "Done? Ain't nobody done, kid. Once you in, you in for life. You know how this works."

Jamal's heart pounded in his chest. He glanced around, his mind racing for a way out. Three of them, and one of him. He couldn't shoot his way out of this. But he also couldn't go down without a fight.

Ghost stepped closer, his hand inching toward his own weapon. "You think you can just walk away from this life? You either die in it, or you die tryin' to escape."

For a moment, the warehouse seemed to close in around Jamal. His thoughts flashed to Keisha, to Tasha, to the life he wanted to build but couldn't seem to reach. He was sick of the game. Sick of the violence, the fear, the constant pull of the streets. But in this moment, staring down Ghost and his crew, it felt like there was no way out.

"Ghost," Jamal said, his voice steady, though his blood raced. "This ain't gonna end how you think it will."

The smile vanished from Ghost's face, replaced by a cold, calculating look. "You got a death wish, kid?"

Jamal didn't answer. Instead, he moved. Fast.

In one swift motion, he pulled the gun from his jacket and fired off a shot, aiming low at the ground near Ghost's feet. The sound exploded in the warehouse, echoing through the empty space. It wasn't meant to hit—it was meant to distract.

And it worked.

Ghost and his boys flinched, and in that split second, Jamal sprinted toward the nearest exit. His heart pounded in his chest as he tore through the dark, his mind laser-focused on getting out of there alive. Behind him, he heard shouts and the deafening crack of gunfire.

Bullets whizzed past him, one grazing his arm, but he didn't stop. He couldn't stop. He burst through the side door of the warehouse and into the night, his legs burning as he sprinted down the alley. The cool night air hit his face, and he pushed himself harder, fueled by adrenaline and the sheer will to survive.

The gunfire behind him faded as he put distance between himself and the warehouse, but he knew this was far from over. Ghost would come for him. Rico had already betrayed him. And Big D—he wasn't going to let this slide either.

Jamal's chest heaved as he slowed his pace, darting through the narrow alleys until he finally stopped behind a dumpster to catch his breath. His mind raced, but one thing was clear—he couldn't keep doing this. The streets were closing in on him, and if he didn't find a way out soon, he'd end up like Trey.

Or worse.

As he leaned against the cold metal of the dumpster, blood seeping from the wound in his arm, Jamal knew he was at a crossroads. He could either keep running, keep trying to survive in a game that was rigged against him, or he could fight for a future that seemed impossible to reach.

But he couldn't do it alone.

For the first time in a long while, Jamal felt a flicker of hope. Tasha had always believed in him, and despite everything, Keisha needed him. Maybe, just maybe, there was still a way out.

But one thing was certain—Ghost wasn't going to let him walk away that easily.

End of Chapter 2

Chapter 3: Cold Realities

The sun barely broke through the gray clouds as morning arrived in Eastwood, casting the streets in a dull, lifeless glow. Jamal's body ached as he leaned against the worn brick wall of an abandoned building, still hidden away from the night before. His mind raced, replaying the events at the warehouse—Ghost's men, Rico's betrayal, the gunfire that had nearly ended his life.

He pressed his hand to the graze on his arm, the blood caked but still fresh. He had escaped death by a hair's breadth, but it wasn't over. Ghost would come for him. He was a walking target now, and running wasn't going to save him.

Jamal knew he needed help, but who could he trust? He had no one left in the streets. **Big D** was a dead end—he'd kill him just as quick if he found out about the setup. Jamal had been walking a

tightrope for years, and now the rope had snapped.

His thoughts shifted to **Keisha**. She was supposed to be at school now, but with the way their mom had been lately, Jamal wasn't sure if she'd even made it out of the house. His gut twisted at the thought of his sister getting sucked into the same hell he'd been living. She deserved better.

He had to fix this.

His phone buzzed in his pocket, and he pulled it out, half expecting a message from one of Big D's goons or, worse, Ghost's crew. But it was a text from **Tasha**. "Hey, where you at? Haven't heard from you. We need to talk."

Jamal's chest tightened. Tasha. She had always been his escape, the one person who made him feel like there was more to life than the streets. She wasn't from Eastwood, didn't know the full depth of the darkness he lived in, but she knew enough to worry.

He hesitated before texting her back.

"I'm good. Just handling some stuff. I'll come by later."

Lying to her felt wrong, but he couldn't drag her into this mess. Not yet. He needed to figure things out first. But even as he tried to keep her at a distance, the thought of seeing her brought a sliver of peace to his chaotic mind.

Pushing off the wall, Jamal glanced down the street. It was time to move. He couldn't stay in one place too long—Ghost's people had eyes everywhere. The streets that had once felt familiar now felt hostile, every corner holding potential danger.

As he started walking, a plan began to form in his mind. He needed to get out of Eastwood. He needed to find a way to disappear before Ghost found him. But more than that, he needed to get Keisha out too. There was no way he was leaving her behind to fend for herself. Not with their mom lost to the drugs and their father long gone.

The problem was money. Jamal had been saving bits and pieces from his runs, trying to put together something for a future beyond Eastwood, but it wasn't enough. Not for two people. He'd need a serious stash to disappear for good.

He checked his phone again, scrolling through contacts, weighing his options. Then, with a heavy sigh, he dialed a number he hadn't used in months.

The line rang twice before a familiar voice answered, rough and low. **"What up, kid?"**

Big Meat. His uncle. His mother's brother. Jamal hadn't spoken to him in a long time, mostly because Big Meat had been out of the game for years. He still had his connections, but he'd made it clear he wanted no part of the new wave of drugs hitting the streets. Especially not fentanyl.

"Unc, it's me, Jamal," he said, his voice tight. "I need your help."

There was a pause on the other end. "What kind of help?"

Jamal took a deep breath, knowing this wasn't going to be easy. "I got caught up with Ghost. It's bad, Unc. I need out."

The silence that followed felt heavy, as though Big Meat was weighing every word carefully. Finally, he spoke. "You know I been out the game for a minute. I told you and your mom a long time ago I wasn't getting involved in this new mess."

"I know, I know," Jamal said quickly. "But I ain't askin' you to get back in. I just need some guidance, some backup. I'm tryin' to get Keisha outta here too."

There was another long pause. Jamal could hear Big Meat breathing, and he imagined him sitting at his kitchen table, a cigarette burning between his fingers, the weight of the world on his shoulders.

"I'll tell you this, Jamal," Big Meat said finally, his voice low and serious. "You want out, you gotta move fast. You gotta get money, get a plan, and get gone. Ghost ain't the type to let you breathe once you cross him. You understand that?"

Jamal nodded, though he knew Big Meat couldn't see him. "Yeah, I get it."

"I'mma send you to someone. He'll get you what you need, but after that, you on your own. I ain't tryin' to get pulled back into this life. I'm done with it."

Jamal felt a flicker of relief. "Thank you, Unc. I appreciate it."

"Don't thank me yet," Big Meat warned. "This ain't a guarantee. If you get caught up again, there ain't nothin' I can do for you."

"I know," Jamal said. "I just need a chance."

Big Meat gave him an address—an old mechanic's shop on the edge of the city, far from Eastwood. He told Jamal to ask for **Manny**, a guy who handled jobs off the grid. No questions asked.

Jamal hung up the phone, a sense of urgency flooding his veins. He had a plan now. It wasn't much, but it was something. First, he had to deal with Manny and get some real cash. Then, he'd figure out how to get Keisha out. Maybe even Tasha, if she'd go with him.

But deep down, he knew it wasn't going to be that simple.

Hours later, Jamal stood outside the mechanic's shop, staring up at the faded sign that read **Manny's Auto Repair**. The place looked run-down, like it hadn't seen a customer in years. It was perfect for what Jamal needed—discreet and out of the way.

He walked through the front door, the bell above it jangling softly. The smell of grease and oil hit him immediately, and the dim lighting cast long shadows across the shop. Behind the counter, a stocky man with a thick beard sat reading a newspaper, not even glancing up when Jamal entered.

"You Manny?" Jamal asked, his voice steady.

The man grunted, folding his newspaper slowly before setting it aside. "Who's askin'?"

"Big Meat sent me," Jamal replied, keeping his tone low. "I need some help."

At the mention of Big Meat, Manny's eyes flickered with recognition. He leaned back in his chair, his expression hardening. "You Meat's nephew?"

"Yeah," Jamal said, feeling the weight of Manny's gaze. "I'm tryin' to get out. Need a way to disappear."

Manny scratched his beard, thinking it over. "That ain't easy, kid. You know how many people come through here askin' the same thing?"

Jamal shifted on his feet, the tension in his body rising. "I'm different. I ain't tryin' to play the game no more."

Manny gave a small nod, though his face remained impassive. "I heard that before. But if Meat sent you, I'll help you. For a price."

Jamal's heart sank. "What kind of price?"

Manny stood up, walking around the counter to face Jamal directly. "A job. You handle it clean, you get the cash you need. But if you mess it up, you're on your own."

Jamal hesitated, his mind racing. He didn't want to do any more jobs, didn't want to be part of this life anymore. But he didn't have a choice. If he was going to get Keisha out, he needed the money.

"What's the job?" Jamal asked, his voice barely above a whisper.

Manny smiled—a cold, calculating smile that made Jamal's skin crawl. "Simple delivery. But you'll be crossing some serious lines. You ready for that?"

Jamal's stomach turned, but he nodded. He was already in too deep. One more job, and maybe— just maybe—he could break free.

End of Chapter 3

Chapter 4: A Thin Line

The rumble of engines and the metallic clank of tools echoed through Manny's garage as Jamal stood in the middle of the dimly lit space, wrestling with the weight of what he was about to do. Manny had given him the details, and it wasn't a simple job, despite the mechanic's casual dismissal of its complexity.

The delivery was to a guy named **Vince**, someone who was deep in Ghost's territory. Vince wasn't just a regular hustler—he ran his own side of the operation, though he kept a low profile. Jamal knew Ghost allowed Vince to operate because he kicked up a healthy cut of his earnings, but Vince had never been loyal to anyone but himself.

Jamal's task was straightforward on paper: deliver a package, take the cash, and get out. But nothing in Eastwood was ever that simple. Jamal didn't know what was in the package, and he didn't ask. That's how people got killed out here. But he had a gut feeling that whatever was in the bag was something Ghost would want to keep his eyes on. Crossing Ghost like this felt like walking through a minefield with a blindfold on.

As Manny handed him the package—a black duffel bag with no markings—Jamal's pulse quickened. It was heavier than he expected, and the weight in his hand felt like a death sentence.

Manny, ever the stoic, barely glanced at him as he gave final instructions. "Vince will be at the old apartment complex off Franklin Street. Third floor, room 308. You make the drop, get your cash, and you're done. Clean and easy."

"Clean and easy," Jamal repeated, his mouth dry. "And if it ain't?"

Manny's eyes flickered, a dangerous glint surfacing for just a moment. "Then it's your funeral, kid. But you handle this right, and you'll get what you need to get gone."

Jamal nodded, his stomach doing flips as he tucked the bag under his arm. He had been in situations like this before, but this one felt different. Maybe it was because he wasn't hustling for himself anymore—this wasn't about making a quick buck to get through the week. This was about Keisha, about getting her out of Eastwood before the streets swallowed her whole.

But no matter how noble his intentions were, he knew the risk. If Ghost got wind of this, if Vince double-crossed him, or if anything went sideways during the drop, he'd be dead before the night was over.

The sun was setting as Jamal left the garage, the sky above painted in shades of orange and pink, the kind of beautiful view that felt completely out of place in a neighborhood like Eastwood. The streets were still alive, though the people who walked them had the look of survivors—hard eyes, quick steps, ready to react to danger at any moment.

Jamal blended into the crowd as he made his way to Franklin Street, moving through alleyways and side streets he knew by heart. The package felt like it was burning a hole in his hand. His mind raced, thinking about every possibility, every way this could go wrong. But then his thoughts drifted to Keisha. She had been quiet the last few days, avoiding him, probably mad that he hadn't been home. Jamal couldn't blame her. He'd been promising her for years that things would get better, that he'd find a way out for both of them. But every time, the streets pulled him back in.

Tonight had to be different. It had to be.

The apartment complex on Franklin Street was a shell of its former self. It had been condemned years ago, but like many places in Eastwood, it still had a few residents, people who didn't care about official notices or building codes. The windows were broken, the walls tagged with graffiti, and the smell of rot and decay filled the air. Jamal paused for a moment, standing in front of the crumbling building, feeling the tension in his muscles.

Third floor, room 308.

His heart thudded in his chest as he made his way inside, careful to keep his head down as he climbed the stairs. The building was eerily quiet, save for the occasional scuttle of rodents or the distant murmur of voices behind closed doors.

When he reached the third floor, he slowed his pace, moving with caution. Room 308 was at the end of the hallway, the door slightly ajar. Jamal felt his pulse quicken again—something about this didn't sit right with him.

He took a breath, steadying himself before pushing the door open a little more. The room was dimly lit, but he could make out Vince's figure lounging in a chair near the window, his back to the door. Two other men were in the room as well, standing near the walls, their hands resting near their waists where Jamal could see the faint bulge of guns under their jackets.

Jamal stepped inside, his grip tightening on the duffel bag. "Vince," he said, his voice cool, though his mind was spinning. "I got your delivery."

Vince didn't turn around right away, instead taking a long drag from the cigarette dangling between his lips. When he finally spoke, his voice was slow, almost lazy. "Jamal, right? Big Meat's nephew?"

"That's right," Jamal said, keeping his distance. "Manny sent me."

Vince stood up slowly, turning to face Jamal with a smirk on his face. He was tall and lean, with sharp features and eyes that never seemed to stop moving. Jamal had seen his type before— always scheming, always looking for an angle. "Hand it over," Vince said, nodding toward the bag.

Jamal didn't move immediately. He had done enough jobs to know when something was off, and right now, his instincts were screaming at him to get out of there. But there was no backing out now.

He stepped forward, tossing the bag onto the table between them. Vince's men didn't move, but Jamal could feel their eyes on him, watching his every move.

Vince unzipped the bag, his eyes narrowing as he peeked inside. He smiled again, but this time it didn't reach his eyes. "Looks like everything's here."

Jamal exhaled, just slightly, ready to collect the cash and get out of there. "Good. Now where's my cut?"

Vince's smile faded as he looked up at Jamal, and the tension in the room grew thicker. One of Vince's men shifted his weight, and Jamal's heart skipped a beat. Something was about to go down.

Vince leaned back, folding his arms. "You're Meat's nephew, right? You ever think maybe you're in the wrong line of work, kid? This isn't for everybody."

Jamal clenched his jaw. "I didn't come here for advice, Vince. I came to make the drop and get my cash. That's it."

Vince chuckled, a low, mocking sound. "I like you. You got guts, but you need to understand something—this ain't just a delivery. When you walk into a room like this, you're making choices. Big ones."

Jamal's eyes narrowed. "What's that supposed to mean?"

Vince's smirk faded entirely, his expression growing cold. "It means Ghost don't take kindly to people moving product behind his back."

The words hit Jamal like a punch to the gut. Ghost? How the hell did Vince know about Ghost's connection to this?

Jamal took a step back, but one of Vince's men blocked his path. Panic surged through him, but he kept his face calm. "Look, I'm just a runner. I don't know anything about Ghost or who's connected to what."

Vince nodded slowly, his gaze hard and calculating. "Maybe you don't, but it don't matter now, does it?"

The room fell into a tense silence, and Jamal's pulse raced. He had to think fast. He could see the way out, but it was blocked by Vince's men. And with the weight of Ghost hanging over everything, it felt like a noose tightening around his neck.

"Here's the deal," Vince said, his voice smooth. "You walk out of here with your cash, or you can forget about ever walking out of here at all. But first, you work for me."

Jamal stared at him, his mind spinning. Work for Vince? That wasn't part of the plan. But right now, his options were shrinking fast, and refusing could mean he wouldn't make it out alive.

He swallowed hard, weighing his choices. Keisha's face flashed in his mind, and he knew that whatever he did now, it had to be for her.

"All right," Jamal said, his voice steady. "I'll work for you."

Vince smiled again, satisfied. He tossed an envelope onto the table. "Smart choice, kid. Now get out of here before I change my mind."

Jamal grabbed the envelope and turned to leave, his heart pounding in his chest. As he stepped out into the hallway, he couldn't shake the feeling that he had just crossed a line he could never uncross. But he had the cash now, and that was all that mattered.

Now, it was time to get Keisha and disappear.

End of Chapter 4

Chapter 5: The Unseen Cost

The streets of Eastwood had changed overnight—or maybe it was Jamal who had changed. As he walked through the city, with the envelope Vince had handed him tucked in his jacket, everything felt heavier, darker. The same cracked sidewalks and crumbling buildings surrounded him, but now, every shadow seemed to hide something sinister. Every corner felt like it had eyes, watching, waiting for him to make a mistake.

The weight of his decision to work for Vince pressed down on his shoulders like a thousand-pound anchor. There was no going back now. He had crossed a line, and no amount of good intentions could erase that. The cash in his pocket, meant to get Keisha out of here, suddenly felt tainted. But as Jamal reminded himself for the hundredth time that night, he didn't have the luxury of regret.

Keisha's life—and his—depended on what he did next.

Jamal made his way back to their small apartment, tucked in the corner of a block that had seen better days decades ago. The walls of the building were stained with years of neglect, and the smell of stale cigarette smoke and mildew hit him as he climbed the stairs. Each step echoed in the silence of the hall, a reminder of the emptiness around him. Most people in Eastwood knew better than to be out at night unless they had business, and if they did, they didn't linger.

He paused outside the door to his apartment, his hand on the knob. For a moment, he felt the urge to turn around and walk away. Maybe it would be better to leave without a word, to spare Keisha from what he'd gotten himself into. But as soon as that thought entered his mind, he pushed it away. Keisha was all he had, and he couldn't abandon her, not now. Not ever.

He opened the door quietly, stepping inside. The apartment was dark, save for the faint glow of the streetlights filtering in through the thin curtains. Keisha was sitting at the small kitchen table, her arms crossed over her chest, her face a mask of anger and hurt. She didn't even look up as he entered, but he could feel the weight of her disappointment hanging in the air.

"Where you been, Jay?" Her voice was low but sharp, each word cutting through the silence.

Jamal closed the door behind him and let out a slow breath, knowing this was coming but still unprepared for it. He walked over to the table, pulling out the envelope and tossing it in front of her. The cash spilled out, a thick stack of bills, more than enough to catch her attention.

Keisha's eyes widened for a second before narrowing again. She stared at the money, then at him, suspicion clear in her gaze. "Where did this come from?"

"I did a job," Jamal said, keeping his voice calm, trying to control the storm brewing inside him. "It was quick. No drama. This'll get us out of here, Keisha. We can leave tonight if we want."

Keisha shook her head, her lips pressed into a tight line. "A job? What kind of job brings in that kind of cash? Don't lie to me, Jay."

He ran a hand over his face, feeling the exhaustion creeping in. "I'm not lying, Keisha. It was a delivery job, that's it. Manny hooked it up."

"Delivery job?" Keisha scoffed, standing up from the table. "I know what kind of deliveries Manny deals in, Jamal. You think I'm stupid? This ain't some fast-food paycheck. This is dirty money."

Jamal flinched at her words, but he didn't argue. She was right, and there was no point pretending otherwise. "I did what I had to do, Keisha. For us. For you. This is our way out."

Keisha's eyes softened for a moment, and he saw the fear lurking behind her anger. "And what happens when they come looking for you, huh? What happens when Ghost or Vince or whoever the hell you're working for decides you're not useful anymore? You think they're just gonna let you walk away?"

Jamal didn't have an answer for that. The truth was, he didn't know how this was going to end. All he could do was focus on the next move, the next step to get them out of Eastwood.

"I can handle it," he said, but even to his own ears, the words sounded hollow.

Keisha sighed and sat back down, her hands trembling slightly as she picked up the stack of cash. "This ain't no fairytale, Jay. We don't get a happy ending just because we want one. This life... it doesn't let go. Not easy."

Jamal sat down across from her, reaching out to take her hand, but she pulled away. The distance between them felt wider than the table separating them.

"I know it's dangerous," he admitted, his voice barely above a whisper. "But I'm doing this for you. For us. We can't stay here, Keisha. Not anymore. The streets... they'll eat us alive if we don't leave now."

Keisha didn't respond right away, her gaze fixed on the pile of money. The silence between them stretched out, heavy and suffocating. Finally, she spoke, her voice soft but laced with fear. "And where are we supposed to go, Jay? What's waiting for us out there?"

"Anywhere but here," Jamal said, leaning forward. "We take this money, and we start fresh. Somewhere far from Eastwood. You can finish school, get a job, do whatever you want. We can be free, Keisha. We just gotta make the move."

She looked up at him, her eyes filled with uncertainty. "And what about you? You think you can just walk away from all this? You think they're gonna let you go?"

"I'll deal with that when the time comes," Jamal said, his voice firm. "Right now, all I care about is getting you out of here. You deserve better than this life, Keisha. We both do."

Keisha stared at him for a long moment, her eyes searching his face as if trying to find some shred of hope in his words. Slowly, she reached out and took his hand, her grip tight. "I'm scared, Jay. I don't want to lose you."

Jamal squeezed her hand, feeling the weight of her fear and his own pressing down on him. "You won't. I promise."

They sat in silence for a while, holding each other's hands, the pile of cash sitting on the table like a ticking time bomb. Jamal knew that this was only the beginning of a much longer journey, one that would be fraught with danger and uncertainty. But for now, they had each other, and that was enough.

The next morning, Jamal woke up before the sun, his mind already racing with the steps he needed to take. Keisha was still asleep beside him, her soft breathing the only sound in the room. He gently slid out of bed, careful not to wake her, and grabbed his phone from the nightstand.

He had one more call to make before they could leave. Jamal scrolled through his contacts until he found **Big Meat's** number. His uncle had been out of the game for a while, but he still had connections, still knew how to make things happen.

Jamal hesitated for a moment before pressing the call button. The phone rang twice before Meat answered, his deep voice gruff and tired. "Jamal. What you want, boy?"

"I need a favor, Unc," Jamal said, keeping his voice low. "I'm trying to get out of Eastwood. For good."

There was a pause on the other end of the line, and Jamal could almost hear the wheels turning in his uncle's head. "That so? You got the kind of money that makes that possible?"

"I do," Jamal said, glancing at the pile of cash still sitting on the table. "But I need help. A way to disappear. Fast."

Meat sighed, a long, weary sound. "You got yourself into some deep shit, didn't you? What you done, boy?"

Jamal didn't want to get into the details. "I just need to know if you can help or not, Unc. I ain't got time to explain."

Another pause, longer this time. Finally, Meat spoke, his voice low and serious. "I can make a call. Get you and your girl out. But it ain't gonna be cheap, and it sure as hell ain't gonna be easy. You ready for that?"

Jamal's heart pounded in his chest, the gravity of the situation sinking in. "Yeah, I'm ready."

"All right," Meat said. "I'll be in touch. But you better be ready to move quick when the time comes."

The line went dead, and Jamal stared at the phone in his hand, his mind racing. This was it. The plan was in motion, and there was no turning back now.

He glanced over at Keisha, still sleeping peacefully in the bed, and a knot formed in his stomach.

He had made his choice, and now they were both caught up in the whirlwind that was about to hit.

But if they could make it through the storm, there was a chance—just a small chance—that they could find the freedom they so desperately needed.

End of Chapter 5

Chapter 6: A Storm Approaching

The next few days passed in a haze of tension and uncertainty. Every hour felt like a countdown, and every sound seemed like it could be the start of something dangerous. Jamal barely slept, and when he did, it was shallow, restless. Keisha noticed, of course, but she didn't say much. Her worry was written all over her face, though. Her usually bright eyes were clouded, her movements slower, more deliberate. They were both waiting, stuck in this limbo between a life they could barely stand and the unknown future that lay ahead.

Eastwood, in the meantime, seemed to go about its usual business. The usual crowd gathered on street corners, the old men playing cards and swapping stories, the younger ones hustling. The junkies shuffling down the block, eyes glassy, looking for their next hit. Life here never really changed, just shifted from one shade of gray to another.

Jamal was growing tired of watching it all from his apartment window, waiting for Meat to come through on his promise. The envelope of cash was still hidden under the mattress, like a ticking time bomb. The weight of it bore down on him every day. He knew they had to move soon, but he had no idea what Meat's plan would involve, or how quickly they'd have to act once the call came.

Late on the third day, the call finally came.

Jamal had been pacing the small living room, half-watching a basketball game on the TV while Keisha studied on the couch. She had her textbooks spread out, trying to focus, but he could tell she wasn't absorbing much. They were both too on edge.

When his phone buzzed on the table, Jamal's heart nearly stopped. He snatched it up quickly and glanced at the screen. It was Meat.

Keisha's eyes followed him as he answered, her expression a mix of hope and fear. Jamal gave her a small nod, trying to reassure her, though he wasn't sure he believed it himself.

"Yeah, Unc?" Jamal's voice came out steadier than he expected.

"I got your way out," Meat's voice was as gruff as ever, though there was an underlying seriousness to it that made Jamal's pulse quicken. "You and your girl need to be ready. We're moving tonight."

Jamal swallowed hard, his free hand clenching into a fist. "How's it gonna work?"

"I made a few calls. Got a driver who's gonna take you out of state, lay low for a bit. He's solid— trustworthy. But you gotta be ready to roll by midnight. Ain't no second chances, you hear me?"

Jamal nodded, even though Meat couldn't see him. "I hear you. Midnight."

"Good," Meat said. "Don't pack too much. Just what you need to get by for a while. I'll send the address where he'll pick you up in a minute. You take that money, and you don't look back. Understood?"

"Yeah, Unc. Thanks." Jamal's voice was tight, the reality of the situation sinking in even deeper. This was real. This was happening.

"You owe me one, kid," Meat said, and Jamal could almost hear the smirk in his voice. "But you get out, you stay out, you hear? Don't come running back to Eastwood. You won't find nothing here but trouble."

Jamal nodded again. "I got it."

"Good luck, Jay. Take care of yourself—and that girl of yours."

The line went dead, and Jamal stood frozen for a moment, the phone still in his hand. His mind raced, processing the gravity of Meat's words. This was it. No more waiting, no more planning. Tonight, they would be gone.

He turned to Keisha, who was watching him with wide eyes, her textbooks forgotten. "We're leaving tonight," he said, his voice steady, though his hands were trembling slightly. "We need to pack. Just the essentials."

Keisha stared at him for a moment, her face a mix of relief and fear. "Tonight?" she whispered.

Jamal nodded, walking over to her and taking her hand. "Yeah. Meat's got someone lined up to take us out of state. We'll be out of here by midnight."

Keisha blinked, the enormity of what he'd just said sinking in. "Out of state... where are we going?" "I don't know yet," Jamal admitted. "But it'll be somewhere safe. Somewhere far from Eastwood. We just need to pack up and be ready."

Keisha bit her lip, standing up from the couch. "I'll get our stuff together."

The next few hours passed in a blur of hurried packing and nervous energy. Jamal and Keisha moved through the apartment, gathering what little they had: clothes, important documents, some cash. Jamal made sure to grab the envelope of money from under the mattress, tucking it into his jacket for safekeeping. Keisha grabbed a couple of her books, unable to leave them behind, even in the face of everything that was happening.

Jamal couldn't shake the feeling that they were being watched. Every time he looked out the window, he half-expected to see someone standing there, waiting for them. The paranoia was getting to him, making his nerves buzz with anxiety.

By the time they had everything ready, it was almost midnight. Jamal had received the address from Meat, a spot a few blocks away where the driver would be waiting. They stood in the middle of their small apartment, bags slung over their shoulders, taking one last look around. "This is it," Keisha said quietly, her voice thick with emotion. "We're really leaving."

Jamal nodded, feeling a lump form in his throat. He had spent his entire life in Eastwood, every memory, good or bad, tied to these streets. But now, it was time to go. Time to start fresh.

"Yeah," he said softly. "We're really leaving."

They walked out of the apartment, closing the door behind them with a finality that echoed through the empty hallways. The night outside was cool and quiet, the city asleep except for the occasional distant sound of a car passing or a dog barking.

Jamal led the way down the block, his senses heightened as he scanned the area. His heart pounded in his chest, every shadow looking like a potential threat. They were exposed out here, vulnerable. He kept a tight grip on Keisha's hand, pulling her close as they made their way to the meeting spot.

When they reached the address Meat had sent, Jamal's pulse quickened. A black sedan was parked on the corner, its engine idling quietly. Jamal glanced around, checking for anything out of the ordinary, but the street was empty.

"This has to be it," he whispered to Keisha.

She nodded, her hand trembling slightly in his.

Jamal approached the car cautiously, his eyes narrowing as he peered through the tinted windows. The driver's window rolled down, revealing a man in his mid-40s, with graying hair and a hardened face that spoke of years in the game.

"You Jay?" the man asked, his voice low and gravelly.

"Yeah," Jamal replied, keeping his voice steady. "You Meat's guy?"

The man nodded. "Get in. We're leaving now."

Jamal opened the back door for Keisha, and she slid in without a word. He followed, pulling the door shut behind him. The interior of the car smelled faintly of cigarettes and leather, the radio playing a low, static-filled tune.

The driver didn't waste any time. As soon as they were in, he pulled away from the curb, the car gliding down the dark streets of Eastwood.

The silence in the car was thick, the weight of what they were doing pressing down on Jamal's chest. Keisha leaned against him, her hand resting on his knee, her grip tight. They didn't speak. There was nothing to say.

As they drove further away from the city, the streets grew emptier, the buildings more spaced out. Jamal stared out the window, watching Eastwood fade into the distance, the lights of the city growing dimmer with each passing mile.

He should have felt relief, but instead, all he could feel was the tension in his gut. They were leaving behind everything they knew, stepping into a future that was uncertain and dangerous. The fear of what lay ahead gnawed at him, but he kept it buried deep, not wanting Keisha to see how scared he really was.

The driver kept his eyes on the road, saying nothing as they crossed the bridge out of Eastwood and into the night. Jamal leaned back in his seat, his mind racing. They were free, for now. But how long would it last?

They drove for what felt like hours, the city now far behind them. Jamal had no idea where they were going, but he didn't ask. He trusted Meat—at least, he hoped he could.

Eventually, the car slowed down, pulling into a small, nondescript motel on the outskirts of a town Jamal didn't recognize. The neon sign flickered in the darkness, casting a faint glow over the parking lot.

"This is where you'll stay for the night," the driver said, his voice breaking the heavy silence.

"Room's already paid for. I'll be back in the morning with your next move."

Jamal nodded, glancing at Keisha. She looked exhausted, her eyes heavy with sleep, but there was still that edge of fear in her expression.

"Thanks," Jamal muttered as they climbed out of the car, grabbing their bags.

The driver didn't respond. He simply nodded and drove off into the night, leaving them standing in front of the motel, the silence pressing in once again.

Jamal led the way to their room, the keys already in his hand from the driver. The room was small and basic, with a single bed, a TV, and a small bathroom. It wasn't much, but it was a temporary haven, a place to rest before the next step.

Keisha dropped her bag on the floor and collapsed onto the bed, her eyes closing almost immediately. Jamal stood by the window, staring out into the darkness, his thoughts a whirlwind of fear, hope, and uncertainty.

They had made it out of Eastwood. But this was just the beginning. The storm wasn't over yet—it was just getting started.

End of Chapter 6

Chapter 7: Pressure Mounts

33

Jamal woke up to the sound of his phone buzzing. The unfamiliar, stuffy motel room was bathed in the pale light of early morning. His body ached, a mixture of tension and exhaustion from everything that had happened the night before. He turned over in bed, careful not to wake Keisha, and reached for his phone on the nightstand. His heart skipped a beat when he saw it was a message from Meat.

"Driver will be back at 10 AM. You two get ready."

Jamal glanced at the small alarm clock next to the bed. It was just after 8. He exhaled slowly and put the phone back down, staring at the ceiling for a moment, trying to get his thoughts together. He was still processing everything—the escape from Eastwood, the money, the danger that hung over their heads like a cloud.

Next to him, Keisha stirred slightly, her soft breathing steady. Her face was peaceful in sleep, but Jamal knew that when she woke up, the reality of their situation would hit her just as hard as it was hitting him. They were out of Eastwood, but that didn't mean they were safe. Not yet.

He sat up in bed, rubbing his face with both hands. The adrenaline from last night had faded, leaving him drained. His mind kept circling back to Hartman, to the mess they had left behind. Jamal knew the cop wouldn't rest until he found them. Hartman didn't just want to hurt them—he wanted to bury them.

Jamal stood up quietly and moved to the window, pulling the curtains back just enough to peek outside. The parking lot of the rundown motel was nearly empty, save for a couple of old cars and a stray cat wandering near a dumpster. The sight was eerily calm, a stark contrast to the storm that raged inside him.

As much as he wanted to believe that Meat's plan would work and that they could disappear, he couldn't shake the feeling that things could still go wrong. Maybe they already had.

By the time Keisha woke up, it was closer to 9 AM. She blinked groggily, sitting up and stretching, her movements slow and heavy.

"Morning," Jamal said softly, leaning against the dresser.

Keisha looked over at him, her expression a mix of confusion and anxiety as the events of the last 24 hours came rushing back to her. "We made it, huh?" she whispered, her voice still thick with sleep.

Jamal nodded. "Yeah, we did. But we gotta keep moving." He hesitated, not wanting to stress her out more than she already was, but he knew they couldn't afford to relax just yet. "Meat's driver is coming back soon. We've got about an hour to get ready."

Keisha sighed, running a hand through her hair. "Where are we even going, Jay?"

Jamal shrugged, looking away for a moment. "I don't know yet. We're just laying low for now, waiting for Meat to send word. He said the driver would take care of everything, but I don't have all the details. We just gotta trust the plan."

Keisha stared at him for a long moment, her dark eyes searching his face for reassurance. "You trust this guy? Meat's driver?"

Jamal hesitated. He didn't know the man from last night, but if Meat had vouched for him, that was the best they could hope for. "I trust Meat," he said finally. "And Meat trusts him. That's gotta be enough right now."

Keisha nodded, though Jamal could see the doubt still lingering in her expression. She stood up slowly, stretching her stiff limbs. "I guess we don't have much choice, huh?"

"No, not really." Jamal moved toward the bathroom. "I'm gonna clean up a bit. Then we'll pack up and get outta here."

Keisha gave him a small, tired smile before turning toward her bag, gathering the few things they had brought with them.

As Jamal stood in front of the small bathroom mirror, splashing cold water on his face, he couldn't help but feel like they were racing against time. No matter how far they went, no matter how carefully they tried to disappear, Hartman's shadow loomed large. He wasn't the kind of man to let something like this slide.

Jamal dried his face and stared at his reflection. His eyes were tired, red from lack of sleep. He hardly recognized the man staring back at him. A part of him wondered what his mom would think if she could see him now. Would she be proud of him for trying to get out, to protect Keisha and himself? Or would she tell him he was fooling himself, that there was no escape from the streets? He shook the thought away. This wasn't the time to get lost in old memories.

By 9:45, they were ready to go. Their bags were packed, and Jamal had checked the room twice to make sure they hadn't left anything behind. Keisha sat on the edge of the bed, her leg bouncing nervously. The room felt claustrophobic, the air thick with unspoken tension.

"We'll be okay," Jamal said, trying to sound more confident than he felt. "Meat's got this planned out. Once we get to where we're going, we can figure out our next steps."

Keisha nodded, though her eyes were distant. "I just want to get out of here. I hate not knowing what's coming."

Jamal understood that feeling all too well. He hated it too. But they were in this now, and the only way out was forward.

A knock on the door made them both jump. Jamal's heart raced as he moved toward it, peeking through the small peephole. It was the driver from the night before, standing there in the same leather jacket, his face unreadable.

Jamal opened the door and nodded. "We're ready."

The driver glanced at Keisha, then back at Jamal. "Good. Let's move. We've got a long drive ahead."

Jamal and Keisha grabbed their bags and followed the man out into the bright morning light. The air outside felt cool and crisp, a stark contrast to the suffocating heat inside the motel room. Jamal took a deep breath, trying to shake off the lingering anxiety that clung to him like a second skin.

The driver led them back to the same black sedan from the night before, and they piled into the back seat once again. As soon as they were settled, the driver pulled out of the parking lot, heading toward the highway.

"Where are we going?" Jamal asked after a few minutes of silence.

The driver didn't take his eyes off the road. "We're heading upstate. There's a safe house where you can lay low for a while. Meat's got it set up. No one knows about it except the people who need to."

Jamal nodded, feeling a small flicker of relief. A safe house. It wasn't a long-term solution, but it would give them some time to figure things out, to plan their next move.

The car sped along the highway, leaving the small town behind. The landscape outside the windows began to change as they drove further north—less urban, more open space. Fields, trees, stretches of road that seemed to go on forever.

Jamal leaned back in his seat, trying to relax, but his mind wouldn't stop racing. Every car that passed them made his heart jump. Every turn in the road felt like it could lead to disaster. He knew he was being paranoid, but he couldn't help it. They were fugitives now, and that changed everything.

Keisha was quiet beside him, staring out the window. Her fingers were intertwined with his, but she hadn't said much since they left the motel. Jamal could sense the weight of everything pressing down on her, just as it was on him.

"You okay?" he asked softly, squeezing her hand.

She turned to him, her eyes heavy with exhaustion. "I don't know, Jay. I just... I didn't think it would feel like this."

"Like what?"

"Like we're running from everything. Like we'll never be able to stop."

Jamal's chest tightened. He knew exactly what she meant. They were running, and even though they had escaped Eastwood for now, the road ahead seemed endless. But he had to keep believing that there was something better waiting for them at the end.

"We'll stop when we're safe," Jamal said quietly. "When we've got a plan. We're not running forever."

Keisha nodded, though her expression didn't change much. "I hope so."

They drove for hours, the sun climbing higher in the sky before eventually beginning its slow descent. By late afternoon, they were deep in the countryside, far from any major city. The landscape was different here—quiet, remote, the kind of place where no one would think to look for them.

Eventually, the driver pulled off the main highway and onto a narrow, winding road that led into a dense forest. The trees loomed high on either side of the car, casting long shadows over the road.

Jamal felt a shiver run down his spine. "Where are we?"

"Almost there," the driver muttered, his eyes scanning the road ahead.

The road twisted and turned for what felt like miles before they finally reached a clearing. A small, weathered cabin sat nestled among the trees, barely visible from the road. It was isolated, hidden away from prying eyes—just the kind of place they needed.

"This is it," the driver said, slowing down in front of a cabin that was at the end of a winding driveway.

The driver pulled the car up to the cabin and parked, shutting off the engine. Jamal and Keisha exchanged glances, their faces reflecting a mixture of relief and unease. The cabin looked like something out of an old horror movie—rustic, isolated, with a sense of desolation that added to the eerie atmosphere.

Jamal stepped out of the car, his legs feeling stiff from the long drive. He stretched, trying to shake off the lingering tension in his muscles. Keisha followed suit, her movements cautious as she took in their new surroundings.

The driver led them to the cabin's front door, which creaked slightly as he opened it. Inside, the cabin was modest but functional—furnished with basic necessities, including a small kitchen area, a couple of armchairs, and a table with four chairs. The place had a lived-in feel, with a few personal touches that suggested it wasn't just a temporary hideout.

"Everything you need is here," the driver said, gesturing around the room. "There's food in the pantry, a few basic supplies. You should be comfortable for a while. I'll check in periodically to make sure you're all right."

Jamal nodded, trying to process the implications of their new environment. "Thanks for everything.

We appreciate it."

The driver gave a curt nod and headed back to the car, leaving Jamal and Keisha alone in the cabin. The silence was palpable, the weight of their situation settling in. Jamal could hear the distant rustle of leaves and the occasional chirp of birds, a stark contrast to the constant hum of city life they'd left behind.

Keisha walked over to one of the armchairs and sank into it, looking around with a mixture of curiosity and apprehension. "It's not much, but it's better than nothing," she said quietly.

Jamal nodded, moving to the window and peering out into the forest. The cabin was well-hidden, but that didn't mean they were completely safe. The woods around them felt both protective and imprisoning. They had a temporary refuge, but it was just that—temporary.

"I'm gonna unpack our stuff and see what we have," Jamal said, moving to their bags and starting to sort through them. He pulled out their clothes, arranging them neatly in a small closet. He also checked the food supplies in the pantry, finding enough to keep them fed for a while. It wasn't much, but it was something.

Keisha stood up and joined him, helping to organize their things. "What now?" she asked, her voice low. "What's our next move?"

Jamal sighed, rubbing his eyes. "We lay low here for a bit. Meat will check in with us soon, and then we'll figure out what to do next. For now, we need to stay under the radar. No going out unless absolutely necessary."

Keisha nodded, though she still looked uneasy. "What if Hartman comes looking for us?"

Jamal swallowed hard. He hadn't wanted to voice that fear, but it was a valid concern. "We have to hope that Meat's plan buys us enough time. If Hartman's looking for us, it's gonna be tough, but we have to keep our heads down and wait for the right moment."

They spent the next few hours settling into their new temporary home. The cabin was small, but it was functional. They made a quick meal from the supplies in the pantry and sat down at the table to eat. The silence between them was heavy, filled with unspoken worries and doubts.

After dinner, Jamal decided to take a walk around the perimeter of the cabin. He wanted to get a sense of their surroundings and make sure there were no obvious security risks. The forest was thick and dense, the trees casting long shadows in the fading light.

As he walked, he couldn't shake the feeling of being watched. The forest seemed too quiet, the air too still. He kept his senses alert, every snap of a twig or rustle of leaves making him jump. It was impossible to know if he was being paranoid or if there was a real threat lurking in the woods.

Jamal made his way back to the cabin, his heart racing. He couldn't afford to let his guard down. They were safe for now, but the danger was far from over.

As night fell, the cabin took on a different atmosphere. The outside world was cloaked in darkness, the only light coming from the small lamp in the living area. Jamal and Keisha settled down in the living room, trying to make the best of their situation.

Jamal had taken out the envelope of money and was examining it, ensuring that everything was still in place. It was a small comfort, knowing they had some resources, but it also served as a reminder of the precariousness of their situation. They needed to be smart with every dollar, careful with every decision.

Keisha had curled up on the couch with one of her textbooks, trying to distract herself from their grim reality. Jamal could see the strain on her face, the worry in her eyes. He wished he could do more to ease her fears, but right now, all he could offer was his presence.

"How's the studying going?" he asked, trying to break the silence.

Keisha looked up from her book, giving him a tired smile. "It's something to do. I guess it helps take my mind off things."

Jamal nodded, though he could see the strain in her expression. "You're doing great, Keisha. Just hang in there a little longer."

The hours dragged on, the quiet of the cabin punctuated only by the occasional creak of the floorboards or the distant call of an owl. Jamal tried to stay alert, his mind racing with thoughts of what might come next. They were in hiding, but the world outside was still full of dangers they couldn't control.

Eventually, exhaustion took its toll, and Jamal found himself sinking into one of the armchairs, his eyes growing heavy. Keisha had already fallen asleep on the couch, her book resting on her chest. He watched her for a moment, feeling a pang of guilt and frustration. This wasn't the life he wanted for her, and he wished he could offer her something better.

Jamal finally allowed himself to close his eyes, drifting off into a fitful sleep. The night seemed endless, filled with fragmented dreams and restless tossing. He knew that come morning, they would have to face whatever came next with renewed determination.

For now, they were safe in their temporary refuge, but Jamal knew that the pressure was mounting. Every decision, every move they made from here on out, would be crucial. The storm was far from over, and the road ahead was uncertain. But they had made it this far, and they had to keep moving forward, no matter how daunting the journey seemed.

End of Chapter 7

Chapter 8: Unseen Threats

Morning arrived slowly, the sunlight filtering through the gaps in the cabin's curtains and casting thin rays of light across the room. Jamal woke up feeling groggy but determined. He rubbed his face and glanced around the small living area. Keisha was still asleep on the couch, her book now resting on the floor beside her.

Jamal stretched, trying to shake off the remnants of a restless night. He had spent most of it tossing and turning, plagued by nightmares and worried thoughts. The sense of being constantly watched hadn't faded, and the isolation of the cabin only heightened his sense of vulnerability.

He got up quietly, careful not to wake Keisha, and made his way to the small kitchen area. He needed to get some coffee brewing to help clear his head. The kitchen was sparsely equipped, but there was a pot, some coffee grounds, and a few mugs. Jamal filled the pot with water and set it on the stove, hoping the familiar routine of making coffee would bring a semblance of normalcy to the situation.

As the coffee brewed, Jamal took a moment to examine their surroundings more closely. He'd been too preoccupied with their escape to fully appreciate the cabin. The furniture was old but well maintained, and there were a few framed pictures on the walls—simple landscapes and generic prints that did little to make the place feel homier.

He wandered around the cabin, checking the locks on the doors and windows. It was important to ensure they were secure, especially with the feeling that someone might be watching. He didn't have any concrete evidence, but it was better to be cautious.

While he was checking the locks on the back door, he noticed a small shed behind the cabin. It was partially obscured by overgrown bushes and looked like it hadn't been used in years. Curiosity got the better of him, and he decided to take a quick look.

The shed was musty and filled with old tools and equipment—nothing particularly useful, but Jamal took note of a few shovels and a rake. The shed could be useful if they needed to clear the area around the cabin or if they needed additional tools for any unforeseen circumstances.

After inspecting the shed, Jamal returned to the cabin and found that the coffee was ready. He poured himself a cup and sat down at the table, trying to collect his thoughts. The morning was eerily quiet, with only the occasional chirp of a bird breaking the silence. It was a stark contrast to the chaos they had left behind.

Keisha stirred as the smell of coffee filled the air. She stretched and blinked sleepily before sitting up and rubbing her eyes. "Good morning," she said, her voice still heavy with sleep.

"Morning," Jamal replied, handing her a mug of coffee. "I thought we could use a little caffeine to start the day."

Keisha took the mug gratefully and sipped it, the warmth seeming to perk her up. "Thanks. I needed that."

Jamal took a sip of his own coffee, savoring the rich, bitter taste. It wasn't much, but it was a small comfort. "We've got some time before the driver checks in. I thought we could go over our plans, see what we need to do next."

Keisha nodded, looking more alert now. "Sounds good. What do we know so far?"

Jamal leaned back in his chair, setting his coffee mug down. "Not much, really. We're supposed to stay here until Meat checks in. Once he does, we'll get more information on what comes next. For now, we need to keep a low profile and stay alert."

Keisha's brow furrowed. "Do you think Hartman is going to come after us here? I mean, this place is pretty remote."

"I hope not," Jamal said, though he didn't sound entirely convinced. "But we can't be sure. Hartman has resources and connections. If he's determined to find us, he might track us down no matter where we go."

Keisha looked around the cabin. "Do you think there's anything we should do to make it safer? I mean, we've got the basics, but we don't know who else might be watching."

Jamal considered her question. "We should be cautious. Check the perimeter again, maybe set up some basic security measures if we can. And keep an eye out for anything suspicious. If we see anything out of the ordinary, we need to be ready to act."

The rest of the morning was spent getting settled. Jamal and Keisha went over the cabin thoroughly, checking every window and door for security. They also spent some time organizing their belongings, making sure everything was in its place.

As the day wore on, they began to feel a bit more comfortable in their temporary home. The quiet of the forest outside was soothing, providing a stark contrast to the chaos they had left behind. Still, the tension never fully left Jamal's shoulders. He was constantly on edge, waiting for something to go wrong.

Around noon, they decided to venture outside for a bit of fresh air. Jamal led the way, carefully scanning the area for any signs of trouble. The woods were dense and secluded, with the only sounds being the rustle of leaves and the occasional call of a bird.

They walked along a small path that led deeper into the forest, keeping their distance from the cabin. It was a chance to stretch their legs and get a better sense of their surroundings. The isolation of the place was both a blessing and a curse—it offered them a refuge from the outside world, but it also left them feeling vulnerable and exposed.

As they walked, Jamal found himself lost in thought. The weight of their situation was heavy on his mind. He knew they couldn't stay here forever, but the idea of moving on without a clear plan was daunting. They needed to figure out their next steps, but that was hard to do with so many unknowns hanging over them.

They stopped by a small stream that ran through the forest, its clear water sparkling in the sunlight. Jamal watched as Keisha knelt down to dip her fingers into the water, her face thoughtful.

"It's peaceful here," she said quietly. "Hard to believe there's so much danger out there."

Jamal nodded, sitting down on a nearby rock. "Yeah. It's like a different world from what we're used to. But we can't forget that danger is still out there. We have to stay sharp."

Keisha looked at him, her expression serious. "I know. I just wish there was a way to make things normal again. I don't want to live like this, always on edge."

Jamal reached out and took her hand, giving it a reassuring squeeze. "We'll get through this. We have to keep believing that. Once we're in a better position, we'll figure out a way to make things right."

The rest of the day passed slowly. They returned to the cabin and spent some time reading and relaxing, trying to make the best of their situation. Jamal kept an eye on the clock, knowing that Meat's driver would be checking in soon.

As evening approached, Jamal found himself growing increasingly restless. The quiet of the cabin was beginning to feel oppressive, the isolation pressing down on him. He needed something to do, something to keep his mind occupied.

He decided to take another walk around the perimeter of the cabin, checking the security once more. The sun was beginning to set, casting long shadows across the forest floor. The world outside seemed to shift from peaceful to ominous as the light faded.

Jamal was deep in thought when he heard a faint noise behind him. He froze, straining to hear. The sound was distant, but it was unmistakable—a faint crackle of twigs, as if someone or something was moving through the forest.

He turned around slowly, scanning the trees for any sign of movement. His heart raced as he listened intently, but the noise had stopped. Jamal took a deep breath, trying to calm his nerves. It could have been an animal, or it could have been something more.

He made his way back to the cabin, his senses on high alert. When he entered, he found Keisha sitting at the table, her book open but her attention focused on him. "Everything okay?" she asked, noticing the look of concern on his face.

"Yeah, I think so," Jamal replied, though his voice was strained. "I thought I heard something outside. Could just be my imagination, but we should stay alert."

Keisha nodded, her expression serious. "We'll keep an eye out. Maybe it's nothing, but it's better to be safe."

The evening dragged on, the quiet of the cabin broken only by the occasional creak of the floorboards or the distant call of a nocturnal animal. Jamal and Keisha tried to relax, but the sense of unease lingered.

As the night wore on, Jamal found it hard to sleep. His mind kept racing, replaying the events of the past few days and worrying about what might come next. The weight of their situation felt heavier with each passing hour.

He lay in bed, staring at the ceiling, trying to quiet the storm of thoughts in his mind. The sound of Keisha's steady breathing beside him was a small comfort, but it didn't fully dispel the anxiety.

Jamal knew they needed a plan, a way to move forward. But for now, all they could do was wait and hope that Meat's driver would bring news that would help them make their next move.

As the first light of dawn began to creep through the windows, Jamal finally drifted into a fitful sleep, his mind still racing with the uncertainty of their future. The storm was far from over, and the road ahead was still fraught with challenges. But for now, all he could do was face each day as it came and hope for a glimmer of hope in the midst of the darkness.

End of Chapter 8

Chapter 9: A New Threat

51

The first light of dawn was a welcome sight for Jamal, who had managed only fitful sleep. He rubbed his eyes and stretched, trying to dispel the lingering fatigue. Keisha was still asleep beside him, her breathing steady and even. The cabin was still cloaked in silence, the world outside bathed in the soft glow of the morning sun.

Jamal decided to get an early start on the day. He tiptoed around the cabin, trying not to disturb Keisha, and headed to the kitchen. The routine of making breakfast provided a small but necessary distraction from his anxious thoughts. He prepared a simple meal of toast and scrambled eggs, hoping that the normalcy of a shared breakfast would offer some comfort.

While the food cooked, Jamal glanced around the cabin. Despite the stress and uncertainty, the cabin had become a small haven of sorts. It was a refuge from the chaos they had left behind, and he was determined to make the most of it. He took a moment to appreciate the stillness of the forest outside, the way the morning light filtered through the trees, casting a golden hue over everything.

As the smell of breakfast filled the air, Keisha stirred and woke up. She stretched and blinked sleepily, then smiled when she saw Jamal preparing food. "Morning," she said, her voice still tinged with sleep.

"Morning," Jamal replied with a smile. "I thought we could use a decent breakfast to start the day."

Keisha got up and joined him at the table, her mood visibly lifted by the aroma of food. "This smells great. Thanks, Jamal."

They ate their breakfast quietly, the meal offering a brief respite from the tension. Jamal used the time to plan their next steps, mentally going over the options and considering their priorities. The quiet of the cabin was soothing, but he couldn't shake the feeling that they were still in danger.

After breakfast, Jamal decided to do another thorough check of the perimeter. He wanted to be absolutely certain that their temporary home was secure. He grabbed a flashlight and a few basic tools from the shed and headed outside.

The forest around the cabin was dense and sprawling, and Jamal carefully made his way through the underbrush. He checked the locks on the doors and windows once again, tightening any screws that seemed loose and making sure everything was in order. He also inspected the area around the cabin, looking for any signs of disturbance or potential vulnerabilities.

As he walked, Jamal's mind wandered back to the unsettling noise he'd heard the previous night. The thought of someone—or something—lurking in the forest was troubling. He kept a keen eye out for any signs of movement, but the forest remained still and quiet.

When he finished his inspection, Jamal returned to the cabin and found Keisha working on her studies at the table. She looked up as he entered, her expression curious. "Everything okay outside?"

"Yeah, it's fine," Jamal said, though he couldn't fully shake the feeling of unease. "Just wanted to make sure everything was secure. Better safe than sorry."

Keisha nodded. "I agree. We should be cautious."

The rest of the morning passed uneventfully. They spent the time organizing their belongings, cleaning the cabin, and trying to make the space as comfortable as possible. Jamal also took some time to read through the papers and documents they had brought with them, looking for anything that might be useful.

By early afternoon, they were both starting to feel restless. The isolation was starting to weigh on them, and they were eager for any news or updates. Jamal had been keeping an eye on the clock, knowing that Meat's driver was supposed to check in soon.

Just as they were beginning to wonder if something had gone wrong, there was a knock at the door. Jamal and Keisha exchanged a quick glance, their hearts racing with anticipation.

Jamal opened the door to find Meat's driver standing on the porch. The driver looked around cautiously before stepping inside. "How's everything going?" he asked, his tone serious.

"It's been quiet," Jamal replied. "We're getting a bit anxious, though. What's the word?"

The driver nodded. "I understand. Things are moving, but it's slow. I've got some information for you, but we need to be careful. Hartman's still looking for you, and he's got resources that make him a formidable opponent."

Jamal felt a pang of worry. "What kind of resources?"

"Connections, surveillance, you name it," the driver said. "He's got eyes everywhere. That's why we need to be extra cautious. Meat's working on getting you some more assistance, but it's going to take a bit of time."

Jamal's frustration was evident. "So what do we do in the meantime?"

"We need to stay under the radar," the driver said. "And there's something else. We've received word that Hartman might be closing in on your location. We don't know for sure, but it's a possibility."

Jamal's heart sank. "What should we do?"

"Keep up the vigilance," the driver advised. "I'll check in regularly and provide any updates as soon as I have them. For now, make sure you stay alert and avoid any unnecessary risks."

The driver left quickly, disappearing into the forest as silently as he had arrived. Jamal and Keisha were left with the weight of his words hanging heavy in the air. The threat was more imminent than they had hoped, and the pressure was mounting.

The rest of the day was spent trying to stay occupied and keep their minds off the growing tension. Jamal and Keisha took turns pacing the cabin and keeping watch. They spent some time reading and discussing their options, but the uncertainty was hard to ignore.

As night fell, Jamal couldn't shake the feeling that something was wrong. The cabin seemed to close in on them, the darkness outside creating a sense of foreboding. The shadows in the forest seemed to grow longer and more menacing.

Around midnight, Jamal was jolted awake by a noise outside. He sat up quickly, straining to hear. The sound was faint but unmistakable—a rustling in the underbrush, as if someone or something was moving around near the cabin.

He reached for his flashlight and quietly got out of bed, careful not to wake Keisha. He grabbed a small tool from the shed and cautiously made his way outside. The forest was dark and silent, the only light coming from the beam of his flashlight.

Jamal moved carefully, scanning the area for any signs of movement. The rustling had stopped, and the forest was still once more. He felt a growing sense of dread, the darkness pressing in around him. He checked the perimeter again, his senses on high alert.

After a tense few minutes, Jamal returned to the cabin, his nerves frayed. He woke Keisha and told her about the noise. She looked concerned but tried to stay calm. "Do you think it's Hartman's people?"

"It's possible," Jamal said, though he wasn't sure. "We need to be ready for anything. I don't want to take any chances."

They spent the rest of the night keeping watch, the tension between them palpable. The forest outside remained dark and silent, but the unease lingered. They had to stay alert and be prepared for whatever might come next.

As the first light of dawn began to filter through the cabin windows, Jamal and Keisha were both exhausted but determined. The threat was real, and they had to stay vigilant. The road ahead was uncertain, and the danger was far from over. But for now, they had to keep moving forward, no matter how daunting the journey seemed.

End of Chapter 9

Chapter 10: The Unraveling

The morning light barely breached the dense canopy of trees surrounding the cabin. Jamal woke up feeling unrested, the lack of sleep taking its toll. He glanced at Keisha, who was still asleep, her face peaceful despite the tension that had been building.

Jamal decided to start the day with a quick check of the perimeter before waking her. The forest was eerily quiet, and the faint morning mist clung to the underbrush. He moved cautiously, every crackle of leaves underfoot setting his nerves on edge. The events of the previous night had only heightened his sense of urgency.

He circled the cabin, his flashlight sweeping over the area. The rustling noise had been unsettling, but it could have been anything—wildlife, the wind, or even just his imagination. Still, he couldn't afford to take any chances. Every window and door was secured, but Jamal wanted to be thorough.

As he worked, he couldn't help but feel a pang of frustration. They were stuck in this remote cabin, isolated from the outside world, and every day seemed to drag on without any concrete information or progress. The waiting was the hardest part, and the uncertainty was a constant weight on his shoulders.

He finished his check and headed back inside, finding Keisha sitting up and rubbing her eyes. "Morning," he said, trying to sound upbeat. "I did another sweep of the area. Everything seems okay, but we need to stay alert."

Keisha nodded, though her eyes betrayed her concern. "I know. It's just hard not to worry, especially with everything that's happened."

Jamal sighed and sat down at the table, grabbing a mug of coffee. "I get it. I'm worried too. But we have to stay focused. Meat's driver should check in again soon, and hopefully, we'll get some updates."

They ate breakfast in relative silence, each lost in their thoughts. The routine of eating together was comforting, but it did little to ease the underlying tension. The cabin's small kitchen, with its simple amenities and modest setup, was a stark contrast to the chaos they had left behind.

After breakfast, Jamal decided to tackle some tasks around the cabin. He organized their supplies, making sure everything was in order and easy to access. He also spent some time looking over the documents they had, searching for any useful information that might help them.

Keisha joined him in organizing their supplies, and they worked side by side in companionable silence. The cabin's small size meant they were often in close quarters, and the shared tasks offered a sense of normalcy amidst the chaos.

Around midday, Jamal and Keisha took a break and decided to venture into the forest once more. The forest was dense and shaded, providing a cool respite from the heat of the day. They followed a small trail that meandered through the woods, hoping that the exercise would help clear their minds and provide a sense of normalcy.

As they walked, Jamal couldn't help but feel a sense of foreboding. The forest, while beautiful, seemed to hold an ominous quiet. The rustling of the leaves and the distant calls of birds were the only sounds, and Jamal was constantly on edge, his senses alert for any signs of trouble.

Keisha seemed to sense his unease and reached out to squeeze his hand. "We'll get through this, Jamal. We have to keep believing that."

Jamal squeezed her hand in return, appreciating the gesture. "I know. It's just hard not to let the worry take over. We need to stay strong and focused."

They continued their walk, the forest seeming to open up as they moved further from the cabin. They found a small clearing with a stream running through it, and they decided to take a break. The cool water and the sunlight filtering through the trees provided a brief sense of peace.

Jamal and Keisha sat on a fallen log and talked about their plans for the future. They discussed their hopes and dreams, trying to find some semblance of normalcy in their conversations. It was a welcome distraction from the constant worry and stress.

As the afternoon wore on, Jamal and Keisha returned to the cabin. They found a message from Meat's driver, left on a note slipped under the door. The note was brief but informative.

"Stay alert. Hartman's people have been seen in the area. They're searching for you. I'll be in touch soon with more information. Be careful."

The note sent a shiver down Jamal's spine. The reality of their situation was setting in once more. Hartman was indeed closing in, and the threat was becoming more immediate.

Jamal read the note aloud to Keisha, her face growing pale as he spoke. "We need to be extra cautious now," Jamal said. "Hartman's people could be anywhere, and we need to be ready for anything."

Keisha nodded, her expression serious. "What should we do?"

Jamal thought for a moment, weighing their options. "We need to secure the cabin and stay on high alert. If Hartman's people are in the area, they might try to make a move soon. We should also start thinking about our next steps—whether we need to relocate or make some other changes."

The rest of the day was spent preparing for the possibility of an imminent threat. Jamal and Keisha double-checked all the locks and windows, making sure that everything was as secure as possible. They also spent some time gathering their belongings and organizing them in case they needed to make a quick escape.

As night fell, the cabin was dimly lit by a single lamp. The shadows seemed to grow longer, and the forest outside felt even more isolating.

Jamal and Keisha settled into their routine of keeping watch, the tension palpable as they waited for any sign of movement.

Jamal tried to keep his mind occupied, but the fear and uncertainty were overwhelming. Every sound seemed amplified in the silence, and the darkness outside felt like a tangible threat. He kept glancing at the clock, anxiously waiting for any updates from Meat's driver.

Keisha was visibly anxious as well, and she tried to stay occupied with her studies. The distraction helped, but the worry never fully left her eyes. They both knew that the danger was real and that they had to be prepared for anything.

Around midnight, Jamal was once again jolted awake by a noise outside. He sat up quickly, his heart racing. The rustling was faint but unmistakable—a sound that seemed too deliberate to be just the wind or wildlife.

He grabbed his flashlight and quietly got out of bed, his mind racing with possibilities. He moved cautiously to the window, peering out into the darkness. The beam of the flashlight cut through the shadows, revealing nothing but the dense forest.

Jamal stepped outside, trying to stay as quiet as possible. The night was cold and still, the only sounds being the occasional snap of twigs underfoot. He moved around the cabin, checking the perimeter once more. The sense of being watched was more intense than ever, and Jamal's nerves were on edge.

After a tense few minutes, he returned to the cabin, finding Keisha awake and waiting. "Did you hear something?" she asked, her voice trembling slightly.

"Yeah," Jamal replied. "I thought I heard something outside. I checked the perimeter, but I didn't see anything."

Keisha looked worried. "Do you think it was Hartman's people?"

"It's possible," Jamal said. "We need to stay on high alert. I'm going to try to get some rest, but we should both keep watch."

They settled back into their makeshift routine of keeping watch, the tension in the cabin palpable. The darkness outside seemed to press in on them, the sense of isolation and danger never far from their minds.

As the night wore on, Jamal tried to quiet his racing thoughts and get some much-needed rest. But the weight of their situation was heavy, and the uncertainty of what lay ahead kept him awake.

The storm was far from over, and the road ahead was fraught with challenges. But for now, all they could do was face each day as it came, hoping for a break in the clouds and the promise of a brighter future.

End of Chapter 10

Chapter 11: The Breakthrough

62

The dawn of the next day was met with a cautious optimism. Jamal and Keisha had managed to get some fitful rest, and the morning light provided a much-needed reprieve from the tension of the previous night. Jamal made breakfast, trying to keep things as normal as possible given their circumstances. Keisha joined him, her demeanor a bit brighter despite the lingering concern.

As they ate, Jamal decided it was time to re-evaluate their situation. They needed to think strategically and prepare for whatever might come next. The threat of Hartman's people closing in was real, and they had to be ready to respond effectively.

"I think we need to come up with a solid plan," Jamal said as he poured himself a cup of coffee. "We can't just keep waiting and hoping for the best. We need to be proactive."

Keisha nodded, her expression thoughtful. "What do you have in mind?"

Jamal took a deep breath. "We need to improve our security, first and foremost. We should make sure the cabin is as fortified as possible. Also, we need to have an escape plan ready in case things get too dangerous."

Keisha agreed. "That sounds like a good idea. We should also think about getting some supplies in case we have to leave quickly."

Jamal and Keisha spent the morning focusing on improving the cabin's security. They reinforced the locks on the doors and windows, making sure there were no weak points that could be exploited. They also gathered their supplies and organized them in a way that would allow for a quick exit if necessary.

As they worked, Jamal couldn't shake the feeling that something was about to change. The constant vigilance and preparation were exhausting, but he knew they had to stay sharp. The sense of unease had become a constant companion, and he was determined to do everything he could to keep them safe.

By early afternoon, Jamal received a message from Meat's driver. It was brief but promising: "I have some updates for you. Meet me at the designated spot at 3 PM. Be discreet."

Jamal shared the message with Keisha, who looked relieved. "Finally, some progress. Hopefully, we'll get some good news."

They decided to head to the meeting spot a bit early to ensure they wouldn't be late. The location was a secluded area near a small lake, chosen for its low visibility and relative safety. Jamal and Keisha packed a few essentials and set out, keeping an eye out for any signs of trouble.

The drive to the meeting spot was tense, each mile adding to their anxiety. They arrived at the location and found a small clearing near the lake, surrounded by tall grass and dense trees. It was the perfect place for a discreet meeting.

They waited in silence, their eyes scanning the surroundings for any sign of the driver. The quiet of the area was almost unnerving, the stillness broken only by the occasional rustle of leaves in the breeze.

After a few minutes, they saw a figure approaching from the edge of the clearing. It was Meat's driver, moving cautiously and scanning the area for any signs of danger. Jamal and Keisha stepped forward to greet him.

The driver gave them a nod of acknowledgment and handed Jamal a folder. "Here's the latest information. We've been able to gather some intel on Hartman's movements and his plans. There's also something else you need to know."

Jamal took the folder and opened it. Inside were several documents and maps, detailing Hartman's known locations and movements. There was also a note with a warning: "Hartman's been getting more aggressive. He's ramping up his search and has increased his resources. Be careful."

Jamal scanned the documents quickly, his mind racing. "This is useful information. It gives us a better idea of where Hartman might be focusing his efforts."

The driver nodded. "Yes, but there's more. We've also identified a potential safe house where you could stay if things get too risky. It's not perfect, but it's better than being exposed in the open."

Jamal looked at the driver with gratitude. "Thank you. This information is a big help. We'll consider relocating if necessary."

The driver gave them a final piece of advice. "Stay alert and don't take unnecessary risks. Hartman is relentless, and his resources are vast. Keep your guard up and be prepared to move if needed."

With that, the driver left, disappearing into the forest. Jamal and Keisha were left with the new information and a renewed sense of urgency. The threat was still present, but the added intelligence provided a glimmer of hope.

They returned to the cabin and reviewed the documents in more detail. The maps and intel gave them a clearer picture of Hartman's movements and the areas where he was most active. They also started planning their potential relocation to the safe house, considering the logistics and preparing for the move if necessary.

The rest of the day was spent organizing their supplies and finalizing their escape plan. They made sure everything was packed and ready to go, ensuring that they could leave quickly if the situation deteriorated.

As night fell, Jamal and Keisha took turns keeping watch, their anxiety tempered by the knowledge that they had a plan in place. The danger was still present, but they felt a bit more prepared and informed.

Despite the ongoing threat, they found a small sense of relief in their preparations. The constant vigilance and uncertainty were exhausting, but the new information and the potential safe house offered a glimmer of hope.

Jamal sat by the window, watching the darkness outside. The forest was still and silent, but he knew that they had to stay alert. The road ahead was still fraught with challenges, but they had taken a crucial step in preparing for whatever might come next.

The storm was far from over, but for now, they had a chance to face it with a bit more confidence and resolve. They would continue to fight against the odds, hoping that their efforts would lead to a brighter future.

End of Chapter 11

Chapter 12: Unraveling Threads

The early morning sun streamed through the small windows of the cabin, casting long shadows across the room. Jamal and Keisha had managed a few hours of restless sleep, their minds still occupied with the recent revelations and the looming threat from Hartman. The new information from Meat's driver had provided some hope, but it also highlighted the gravity of their situation.

Jamal woke first and decided to take advantage of the quiet morning to review the documents in more detail. He spread the maps and intel across the kitchen table, studying them with intense concentration. The maps detailed Hartman's known locations and potential areas of interest, while the documents included profiles of Hartman's associates and recent activities.

Keisha joined him as he worked, her eyes heavy with sleep but focused. "How's it looking?" she asked, her voice soft but concerned.

Jamal glanced up and sighed. "The intel is detailed, but it's also overwhelming. Hartman's operations are extensive, and he's got a lot of resources at his disposal. We need to stay sharp." Keisha nodded and took a seat at the table, her expression serious. "What's our next move?"

Jamal pointed to a marked location on the map. "The safe house is here. It's about a two-hour drive from here, and it's in a more secluded area. If things get too dangerous, we'll need to relocate there."

Keisha studied the map and then looked at Jamal. "Do we know anything about the safe house itself? Is it secure?"

"According to the information, it's not perfect, but it's better than being exposed in the open. It has basic amenities and is relatively hidden. We should still be cautious and make sure it's safe before fully committing."

They spent the next few hours preparing for the possibility of relocation. They packed their essential belongings and organized their supplies, making sure everything was ready for a quick move if necessary. The process was methodical and tense, each item packed with a sense of urgency.

Around noon, Jamal decided it was time to take a break and get some fresh air. He and Keisha ventured outside, taking a walk through the forest surrounding the cabin. The forest was a stark contrast to the tension they felt; its tranquility offered a brief respite from the anxiety that had become their constant companion.

As they walked, Jamal and Keisha discussed their plans and options. They talked about their hopes for the future, their fears, and the steps they needed to take to stay safe. The conversation helped to clear their minds and provided a small sense of normalcy.

After their walk, they returned to the cabin and resumed their preparations. The sense of urgency was palpable, and they knew that any delay could be dangerous. They finished packing and made sure their escape route was planned out.

Later in the afternoon, they received another message from Meat's driver. It was short but contained a critical update: "Hartman's team is moving closer. They're conducting searches in the area. Be prepared to leave at a moment's notice."

The message intensified their sense of urgency. Jamal and Keisha reviewed their preparations, making final adjustments to their plans. They checked their supplies, double-checked their packed items, and reviewed their route to the safe house.

As evening approached, Jamal and Keisha continued their vigil. The threat of Hartman's team searching the area added to their anxiety. Every sound outside seemed amplified, and the quiet of the cabin felt oppressive.

Around 7 PM, Jamal decided to take one last check of the perimeter. He ventured outside, moving cautiously through the darkening forest. The shadows were long, and the dense trees seemed to close in around him.

As he moved, Jamal noticed a faint light in the distance, possibly from a vehicle. He paused and tried to discern the source. The light seemed to move intermittently, and Jamal's heart raced with apprehension. He returned to the cabin and shared his observation with Keisha.

"I saw a light in the distance," Jamal said, his voice tense. "It could be a vehicle or someone searching the area. We need to be ready."

Keisha's face paled. "Do you think it's Hartman's people?"

"It's possible," Jamal replied. "We need to stay alert and be prepared to move if necessary."

The night wore on with a heightened sense of tension. Jamal and Keisha took turns keeping watch, their nerves frayed by the uncertainty. The threat of Hartman's team moving closer added to their anxiety, and they remained on edge, ready to act at a moment's notice.

Around midnight, Jamal heard the faint sound of voices outside. He tensed and signaled to Keisha, who quickly joined him at the window. They listened intently, trying to make out the conversation.

The voices were distant but unmistakable, and Jamal's heart sank as he realized that someone was indeed searching the area. He and Keisha moved silently, gathering their things and preparing for a possible evacuation.

Jamal took one last look around the cabin, ensuring they had everything they needed. He felt a pang of regret as he glanced at the place that had been their refuge. The cabin had provided a brief respite from their troubles, but now it was time to move on.

As they prepared to leave, Jamal and Keisha gathered their belongings and carefully made their way to their vehicle. The darkness of the forest seemed to press in on them, and every rustle of leaves and snap of twigs heightened their anxiety.

They drove cautiously through the forest, following the route to the safe house. The road was winding and treacherous, and Jamal remained focused on the task at hand. The safety of their new location was crucial, and they needed to stay alert.

As they approached the safe house, Jamal and Keisha felt a mix of relief and apprehension. The safe house was a modest, single-story building nestled in a secluded area. It was well-hidden from the road and surrounded by dense trees, offering a degree of privacy and security.

Jamal parked the vehicle and they both stepped out, surveying their new surroundings. The safe house seemed to be in good condition, and Jamal felt a glimmer of hope. They carefully approached the building and checked it for any signs of tampering or damage.

Inside, the safe house was sparsely furnished but functional. It had the basics—a small kitchen, a living area, and a couple of bedrooms. Jamal and Keisha set about unpacking their belongings and making the place feel as comfortable as possible.

By the time they finished settling in, it was well past midnight. They were exhausted but relieved to have reached a new, safer location. The threat of Hartman's team was still present, but the safe house offered a new layer of protection.

Jamal and Keisha took a moment to rest, their minds still racing with the events of the past few days. The move had been stressful, but they were hopeful that the safe house would provide the security they needed.

As they prepared for bed, Jamal couldn't shake the feeling that they were still on the edge of danger. The threat from Hartman was far from over, and the road ahead remained uncertain. But for now, they had a new place to call home, and that offered a small measure of hope.

They settled into their new surroundings, the quiet of the safe house a welcome change from the constant tension of the cabin. The storm was far from over, but they had taken a crucial step in their fight for safety and survival.

End of Chapter 12

Chapter 13: Shadows and Secrets

73

The first light of dawn crept through the windows of the safe house, casting a soft glow over the room. Jamal woke to the sound of birds chirping outside, a welcome change from the oppressive silence of the forest. Despite the morning's tranquility, a sense of unease lingered, a constant reminder of the danger they had narrowly escaped.

Jamal stretched and then made his way to the small kitchen. He needed to start the day with a plan. The safe house offered them temporary refuge, but the reality of their situation was still daunting. Hartman's threat was real and persistent, and Jamal knew they needed to be strategic in their next steps.

Keisha joined him shortly, her eyes still heavy with sleep but her demeanor resolute. "How are you feeling?" she asked, rubbing her eyes as she sat down at the kitchen table.

Jamal poured two cups of coffee and handed one to Keisha. "Better than last night, but we still have a lot to figure out. We need to get a better sense of our surroundings and make sure this place is secure."

Keisha nodded, taking a sip of her coffee. "Agreed. We should also start planning our next moves. We can't stay here forever, and we need to be prepared for anything."

They spent the morning familiarizing themselves with the safe house. Jamal checked every door and window, ensuring that they were secure and that there were no weak points. He also inspected the surrounding area, looking for potential vulnerabilities or areas where they might need to be extra cautious.

The safe house was located in a remote area, surrounded by dense woods and rolling hills. It was isolated enough to offer privacy and protection, but that also meant they were further away from any immediate help or resources. Jamal noted the various escape routes and potential hiding spots, making mental notes of where they might go if they needed to leave quickly.

Keisha busied herself with organizing their supplies and setting up their living space. She arranged their belongings in a way that would make it easy to find what they needed and prepared the small kitchen for daily use. Her efforts helped to create a sense of normalcy in the midst of their chaotic situation.

By midday, Jamal and Keisha had settled into a routine. They took turns keeping watch, monitoring the area for any signs of trouble. The safe house, while more secure than the cabin, still required constant vigilance. Every sound and movement outside was scrutinized, and they both remained on high alert.

Jamal decided it was time to review the documents they had received from Meat's driver. He spread them out on the kitchen table and studied them closely. The maps and profiles provided valuable information, but they also highlighted the extent of Hartman's operations.

Keisha joined him at the table, her curiosity piqued. "What's the latest?"

Jamal pointed to a marked area on the map. "This is where Hartman's team has been most active. According to the intel, they're focusing their search efforts here and here." He traced the locations with his finger.

Keisha frowned as she looked over the documents. "That's close to where we were. Do you think they've already been here?"

"It's possible," Jamal replied. "We need to be cautious and keep a low profile. If Hartman's team is searching the area, they might be getting closer."

They spent the afternoon discussing their options and planning their next steps. They considered various scenarios and potential responses, trying to anticipate Hartman's moves and prepare for any contingencies.

As evening approached, Jamal and Keisha decided to take a break and get some fresh air. They ventured outside and walked around the perimeter of the safe house, enjoying the peaceful surroundings but remaining vigilant. The forest was serene, with the gentle rustling of leaves and the distant sound of a brook adding to the sense of calm.

During their walk, Jamal and Keisha talked about their future plans and the steps they needed to take to stay safe. The conversation provided a brief respite from the constant tension and allowed them to refocus on their goals.

As they returned to the safe house, they noticed something unusual—a small, inconspicuous object near the edge of the property. It was a metal casing, partially buried in the dirt. Jamal carefully examined it, his mind racing with possibilities.

"This looks like it might be some kind of signal device or tracking equipment," Jamal said, showing the casing to Keisha. "We need to be careful. It could mean that someone has been monitoring this area."

Keisha's eyes widened with concern. "What do we do?"

Jamal carefully pocketed the casing. "We'll keep it for now and see if we can get any information from it. For now, let's stay alert and continue with our preparations."

As night fell, Jamal and Keisha resumed their watch. The safe house was quiet, but the darkness outside seemed to heighten their sense of unease. The threat from Hartman's team was still present, and the need for constant vigilance remained.

Jamal took some time to review the documents and maps again, trying to identify any patterns or additional information that might be useful. The intel they had was valuable, but it was clear that they needed to stay one step ahead of Hartman.

Keisha, meanwhile, worked on organizing their supplies and making sure everything was in order. She also spent some time researching potential escape routes and safe locations, preparing for the possibility that they might need to leave the safe house in a hurry.

As the night wore on, Jamal and Keisha exchanged stories and talked about their hopes for the future. The conversations helped to alleviate some of the tension and provided a brief sense of normalcy.

In the early hours of the morning, Jamal received a call from Meat's driver. The call was brief but urgent. "Hartman's team is getting closer. We've received reports that they're intensifying their search efforts. Be prepared to move if necessary."

Jamal relayed the message to Keisha, and they both knew that the situation was becoming more critical. They quickly reviewed their plans and made final preparations, ensuring that they were ready for a possible evacuation.

As dawn approached, Jamal and Keisha were on edge, their nerves frayed by the uncertainty of their situation. The safe house had provided temporary relief, but the threat from Hartman was a constant reminder of the danger they faced.

With their preparations complete, Jamal and Keisha took one last look around the safe house. They had made the best of their situation, but the road ahead remained uncertain. The storm was still raging, and they had to stay vigilant and prepared for whatever might come next.

The quiet of the early morning was a stark contrast to the tension they felt, but they knew that they had to stay strong and focused. The fight for their safety and survival was far from over, and they would continue to face each day with determination and resolve.

End of Chapter 13

Chapter 14: The Gathering Storm

The morning broke with an eerie calm, the safe house bathed in the soft, golden light of the rising sun. Despite the tranquility outside, Jamal and Keisha were far from relaxed. The urgency of the situation weighed heavily on them as they prepared for the possibility of a swift departure.

Jamal woke early, his mind already racing with thoughts of their next steps. He had barely slept, the constant vigilance and anticipation of trouble keeping him awake. The threat from Hartman's team was looming larger with each passing day, and the need to stay ahead of their pursuers was becoming more critical.

He quietly made his way to the kitchen, determined to start the day with a clear plan. He brewed a pot of coffee, the familiar aroma offering a momentary comfort amidst the tension. As he sipped his coffee, he reviewed the maps and documents once again, searching for any overlooked details that could provide an advantage.

Keisha joined him shortly, her face a mixture of exhaustion and resolve. "Morning," she said, her voice tinged with fatigue. "Any updates?"

Jamal shook his head. "Nothing new, but we need to be ready for anything. Hartman's team is closing in, and we need to have a plan for every possible scenario."

Keisha nodded, her expression thoughtful. "I've been thinking about our options. We need to consider both short-term and long-term strategies. What if we need to stay on the move for a while?"

"That's a good point," Jamal agreed. "We should plan for the possibility of relocating frequently.

We need to identify safe spots and make sure we have enough supplies to last if we're on the road."

They spent the morning organizing their supplies and reviewing their escape routes. Jamal compiled a list of potential safe locations, both in terms of hiding spots and places where they could find temporary refuge. They also gathered additional provisions, ensuring they had enough food, water, and essentials to last if they had to leave in a hurry.

By midday, Jamal and Keisha were deep in their preparations. They reviewed their communication options, ensuring they had reliable means to stay in touch with Meat's driver and other contacts.

The potential for needing immediate assistance made this an important aspect of their planning.

Jamal decided it was time to further investigate the metal casing they had found near the property. He took it out and examined it closely, trying to determine its purpose and potential significance. Keisha joined him, her curiosity piqued.

"This thing looks like it could be some sort of tracking device or signal transmitter," Jamal said, holding up the casing. "If Hartman's people are using this to monitor the area, we need to be extra cautious."

Keisha nodded. "Do you think there's any way to trace it or figure out how it works?"

Jamal considered the question. "I'm not sure, but I think it's worth a try. If we can figure out how it operates, it might give us some insight into Hartman's methods and intentions."

They spent the next few hours examining the casing and trying to decipher its components. It was a slow process, and their progress was hampered by their limited tools and knowledge. Despite the challenges, Jamal remained determined to uncover any useful information.

As evening approached, Jamal and Keisha decided to take a break from their work and get some fresh air. They ventured outside once again, walking around the perimeter of the safe house and enjoying the peaceful surroundings. The tranquility of the forest was a stark contrast to the anxiety they felt, and the respite was a welcome relief.

During their walk, they came across a small, hidden path that led deeper into the woods. Jamal and Keisha followed the path for a short distance, intrigued by the possibility of discovering something useful. The path eventually led to a small clearing, where they found a weathered wooden cabin.

The cabin was old and dilapidated, but it appeared to be abandoned. Jamal and Keisha cautiously approached, their senses alert for any signs of danger. They inspected the cabin and found it to be empty, but it offered some interesting possibilities.

"This could be another potential hiding spot," Jamal said, surveying the area. "It's isolated and hidden, which could make it a useful location if we need to move quickly."

Keisha agreed. "It's worth keeping in mind. We should also consider whether it's secure enough to use as a temporary refuge."

They took note of the cabin's location and made plans to revisit it if necessary. The discovery provided a small glimmer of hope, offering another option in their quest for safety.

As night fell, Jamal and Keisha returned to the safe house and resumed their preparations. The sense of urgency was palpable, and they knew that every moment counted. The threat from Hartman's team was ever-present, and they needed to stay vigilant.

Jamal continued his examination of the metal casing, trying to extract any useful information. His efforts were met with limited success, but he remained determined to uncover its secrets. The casing was a potential link to Hartman's operations, and understanding its purpose could provide valuable insights.

Keisha worked on organizing their supplies and preparing for the possibility of an immediate departure. She made sure everything was packed and ready to go, ensuring that they could leave quickly if the situation required it.

As the hours ticked by, Jamal and Keisha took turns keeping watch. The quiet of the safe house was a stark contrast to the tension they felt, and every sound outside was scrutinized with a heightened sense of alertness.

Around midnight, Jamal received another call from Meat's driver. The news was both alarming and urgent. "Hartman's team is closing in faster than expected. We've received reports that they're conducting searches in multiple areas. You need to be ready to move immediately."

Jamal relayed the message to Keisha, and they both knew that their situation had become even more precarious. They quickly reviewed their plans and made final preparations, ensuring that they were ready for a swift evacuation.

With their preparations complete, Jamal and Keisha took one last look around the safe house. The security of their new location was still uncertain, and the threat from Hartman's team remained a constant worry. But they had made the best of their situation, and they were ready to face whatever challenges lay ahead.

The quiet of the early morning was a brief respite from the tension, but it also served as a reminder of the ongoing danger. Jamal and Keisha knew that their fight for safety and survival was far from over, and they would continue to face each day with determination and resolve.

As they settled in for the night, the storm of uncertainty continued to swirl around them. But with each step, they moved closer to finding a path to safety and reclaiming their lives from the shadows of their pursuers.

End of Chapter 14

Chapter 15: Breaking Points

The first hint of dawn crept through the thin curtains of the safe house, casting a dim light across the room. Jamal and Keisha were already awake, their sleep interrupted by the relentless weight of their situation. Despite their exhaustion, they knew that every moment was crucial in their struggle to stay ahead of Hartman's team.

Jamal was the first to rise, his mind racing with thoughts of their next steps. The previous night's news had only heightened their sense of urgency. Hartman's team was closing in faster than anticipated, and the safe house was no longer as secure as they had hoped. They needed to act quickly and decisively.

He moved quietly through the kitchen, preparing a quick breakfast for them both. The smell of coffee and the sizzle of eggs provided a small comfort, a fleeting reminder of normalcy in their chaotic lives. Keisha joined him shortly, her eyes still heavy with sleep but her demeanor resolute.

"Morning," Keisha said, taking a seat at the table. "Any new updates?"

Jamal shook his head, handing her a cup of coffee. "Nothing concrete yet, but we need to be ready for anything. We should finalize our plans for the day and prepare for a possible evacuation."

Keisha nodded, taking a sip of her coffee. "I agree. We need to be prepared for the worst-case scenario. Let's review our options and make sure we have everything in place."

After breakfast, Jamal and Keisha focused on finalizing their plans. They reviewed their escape routes and made sure their supplies were packed and ready to go. The sense of urgency was palpable as they worked, each task carried out with a meticulous attention to detail.

Jamal checked the maps and documents once again, searching for any additional information that might be useful. He made notes of potential safe locations and ensured that their communication options were secure. The pressure to stay ahead of Hartman's team was immense, and Jamal felt the weight of responsibility heavy on his shoulders.

Keisha, meanwhile, continued organizing their supplies and preparing for a possible move. She made sure they had enough food, water, and essentials to last if they had to leave in a hurry. Her efficiency and attention to detail were crucial in their preparations, and Jamal appreciated her efforts.

As they worked, they occasionally glanced at the metal casing they had found. Jamal had managed to identify some of its components, but its full purpose remained a mystery. He hoped that further examination might yield some useful information.

Around midday, Jamal and Keisha decided to take a break and get some fresh air. They ventured outside, walking around the perimeter of the safe house and enjoying the serene surroundings. The forest was quiet, its beauty a stark contrast to the tension they felt.

During their walk, they discussed their plans and the potential challenges they might face. The conversation provided a brief respite from the constant stress and allowed them to refocus on their goals.

As they returned to the safe house, Jamal noticed a figure in the distance. It was a person, moving cautiously through the woods. His heart raced as he considered the possibility of an encounter. He quickly signaled to Keisha, and they moved to a vantage point where they could observe the stranger without being seen.

The figure approached the safe house, moving with deliberate care. Jamal and Keisha watched from their hiding spot, their senses on high alert. The figure appeared to be searching the area, but their intentions remained unclear.

After a few tense minutes, the figure turned and began to move away from the safe house. Jamal and Keisha waited until they were sure the stranger was gone before emerging from their hiding spot.

"That was close," Keisha said, her voice tense. "Do you think it was Hartman's team?"

Jamal shook his head, still processing the encounter. "I'm not sure, but it's definitely a concern.

We need to be even more vigilant. Let's keep an eye out for any other suspicious activity."

The rest of the day was spent on high alert. Jamal and Keisha continued their preparations, making sure everything was in order. They reviewed their plans and discussed their options, trying to anticipate any potential problems.

As evening approached, they received another call from Meat's driver. The news was urgent. "Hartman's team is ramping up their search efforts. We've received reports that they're intensifying their efforts in the area. You need to be ready to move at a moment's notice."

Jamal relayed the message to Keisha, and they both understood the gravity of the situation. They quickly made final preparations for a possible evacuation, ensuring that they were ready for any scenario.

With their preparations complete, Jamal and Keisha took one last look around the safe house. The security of their location was still uncertain, and the threat from Hartman's team remained a constant concern. But they had done everything they could to prepare, and now it was a matter of staying vigilant and ready for whatever might come next.

As night fell, Jamal and Keisha settled into a routine of keeping watch. The quiet of the safe house was a stark contrast to the tension they felt, and every sound outside was scrutinized with a heightened sense of alertness. They took turns monitoring the area, their nerves frayed by the uncertainty of their situation.

Around midnight, Jamal received a call from Meat's driver with more alarming news. "Hartman's team is conducting searches in multiple areas. We've received reports that they're getting closer to your location. You need to be prepared to leave immediately."

Jamal shared the news with Keisha, and they both knew that their time at the safe house was running out. They quickly reviewed their plans and made final adjustments, ensuring that they were ready for a swift departure.

With their preparations complete, Jamal and Keisha took one last look around the safe house. The security of their location was still uncertain, and the threat from Hartman's team remained a constant concern. But they had done everything they could to prepare, and now it was a matter of staying vigilant and ready for whatever might come next.

The quiet of the early morning was a brief respite from the tension, but it also served as a reminder of the ongoing danger. Jamal and Keisha knew that their fight for safety and survival was far from over, and they would continue to face each day with determination and resolve.

As they prepared to leave, the storm of uncertainty continued to swirl around them. The path ahead was fraught with challenges, but they were determined to navigate it with courage and resilience. The safe house had been a temporary refuge, but the real fight was just beginning.

End of Chapter 15

Chapter 16: The Breaking Point

The early morning light filtered through the trees, casting long shadows across the safe house. Jamal and Keisha were up before dawn, their nerves on edge as they prepared for what might be their final moments at this location. The urgency of the situation had reached a fever pitch, and they knew that every decision they made could be crucial to their survival.

Jamal's mind was racing. The latest news from Meat's driver had intensified their sense of urgency. The information that Hartman's team was closing in faster than anticipated meant that they had to be ready to move at a moment's notice. Their plans had to be flawless, and every detail needed to be accounted for.

Keisha was equally focused, her movements precise and deliberate as she packed their supplies. She worked with a sense of determination, knowing that their next actions would determine their safety. The weight of their situation was heavy, but she refused to let it show.

"Everything's packed and ready," Keisha said, her voice steady despite the tension. "What's the plan for today?"

Jamal took a deep breath, trying to calm his racing thoughts. "We need to be prepared for an immediate evacuation. We'll stay alert and monitor the area closely. If we get the signal, we leave without hesitation."

Keisha nodded, her eyes meeting Jamal's with a shared understanding. "I'll keep an eye on the surroundings while you review the maps and documents one more time. Let's make sure we're fully prepared."

As the morning wore on, Jamal and Keisha carried out their final preparations. Jamal rechecked their escape routes, ensuring that he had a clear understanding of their options. He marked potential safe locations on the map and reviewed the communications plan, making sure they had reliable means of staying in touch with their contacts.

Keisha organized their supplies, ensuring that everything was packed efficiently and ready for a quick departure. She took special care to include essential items such as first aid supplies, additional food and water, and important documents.

The tension in the safe house was palpable. Every noise outside was scrutinized, and Jamal and Keisha remained on high alert. The feeling of being watched was constant, a reminder of the ever present threat from Hartman's team.

Around noon, Jamal and Keisha decided to take a break and grab some fresh air. They walked around the perimeter of the safe house, their senses heightened as they surveyed their surroundings. The forest was quiet, but the stillness only added to their unease.

During their walk, Jamal noticed a few small changes in the area. The ground was disturbed in several places, and there were signs of recent activity. His heart raced as he considered the possibility that Hartman's team might be closer than they had anticipated.

"Look at this," Jamal said, pointing out the disturbed ground. "This wasn't here before. It could mean someone has been here recently."

Keisha's eyes widened with concern. "Do you think they're onto us?"

"It's possible," Jamal replied, his mind racing with possibilities. "We need to be extra cautious.

Let's head back to the safe house and review our plans."

Back at the safe house, Jamal and Keisha quickly resumed their preparations. The signs of recent activity had heightened their sense of urgency, and they needed to be ready for any eventuality. They reviewed their escape routes again, making sure they had multiple options in case one was compromised.

Jamal also decided it was time to further investigate the metal casing they had found. He set up a makeshift workstation and continued his examination, hoping to uncover any useful information. Keisha joined him, offering her assistance as they worked.

"This thing is more complex than I thought," Jamal said, his frustration evident. "It's got several components that I can't quite identify. I'm hoping that if we can figure out its purpose, it might give us some insight into Hartman's operations."

Keisha nodded, her expression focused. "Let's keep at it. Even if we don't get a definitive answer, we might find something useful."

As evening approached, Jamal and Keisha received another call from Meat's driver. The news was troubling. "Hartman's team has intensified their search efforts even further. They're conducting searches in multiple locations, and it's becoming more difficult to predict their movements. You need to be prepared to move immediately."

Jamal relayed the message to Keisha, and they both understood the gravity of the situation. They quickly made final adjustments to their plans, ensuring that they were ready for a swift departure if necessary.

With their preparations complete, Jamal and Keisha took one last look around the safe house. The security of their location was still uncertain, and the threat from Hartman's team remained a constant concern. But they had done everything they could to prepare, and now it was a matter of staying vigilant and ready for whatever might come next.

As night fell, Jamal and Keisha settled into their routine of keeping watch. The quiet of the safe house was a stark contrast to the tension they felt, and every sound outside was scrutinized with a heightened sense of alertness. They took turns monitoring the area, their nerves frayed by the uncertainty of their situation.

Around midnight, Jamal received another call from Meat's driver. The urgency in the driver's voice was palpable. "Hartman's team is closing in rapidly. They've intensified their search efforts, and it's only a matter of time before they find your location. You need to be ready to leave immediately."

Jamal shared the news with Keisha, and they both knew that their time at the safe house was running out. They quickly reviewed their plans and made final preparations, ensuring that they were ready for a swift evacuation.

With their preparations complete, Jamal and Keisha took one last look around the safe house. The security of their location was still uncertain, and the threat from Hartman's team remained a constant concern. But they had done everything they could to prepare, and now it was a matter of staying vigilant and ready for whatever might come next.

The quiet of the early morning was a brief respite from the tension, but it also served as a reminder of the ongoing danger. Jamal and Keisha knew that their fight for safety and survival was far from over, and they would continue to face each day with determination and resolve.

As they prepared to leave, the storm of uncertainty continued to swirl around them. The path ahead was fraught with challenges, but they were determined to navigate it with courage and resilience.

The safe house had been a temporary refuge, but the real fight was just beginning.

Jamal and Keisha knew that they had to stay one step ahead of their pursuers. The battle for their safety was far from over, and they were prepared to face whatever challenges lay ahead with unwavering resolve.

End of Chapter 16

92

The predawn hours were heavy with anticipation. Jamal and Keisha were in constant motion, their preparations reaching a fever pitch. The threat from Hartman's team was now a looming, omnipresent force, casting a shadow over every decision they made. As they gathered their belongings, the air was thick with tension, each sound outside magnified by their heightened senses.

Jamal and Keisha had spent the night in a state of anxious vigilance. Despite the small comforts they had created for themselves, the reality of their situation was impossible to ignore. Every creak of the floorboards and rustle of leaves outside seemed to signal an imminent threat. They moved with practiced efficiency, their every action measured and deliberate.

Jamal took a final inventory of their supplies. The backpack was packed tight, bulging with essentials—food, water, medical supplies, and a few personal items. He had added an emergency toolkit and a portable charger, knowing that their access to reliable power might become unpredictable. He checked the maps again, ensuring that they had all possible routes planned out. The metal casing, which they had hoped to analyze more thoroughly, had been set aside, its significance still unclear but its presence a constant reminder of the danger they faced.

Keisha, meanwhile, was busy with last-minute checks. She meticulously reviewed their communication devices, making sure that each was fully charged and functioning. She had also prepared a small first-aid kit with everything they might need in case of an emergency—bandages, antiseptic, pain relievers, and a few doses of antibiotics. The stakes were high, and being unprepared was not an option.

As the first light of day began to pierce through the trees, Jamal and Keisha took a moment to gather their thoughts. The calm of the forest was in stark contrast to the chaos that was unfolding in their lives. They knew that the safe house was no longer a viable option, and the reality of their situation was sinking in.

Jamal and Keisha decided to use the few hours of daylight to their advantage. They moved methodically through their final checks, ensuring that they had accounted for every detail. Jamal reviewed their escape routes once again, his mind racing through potential scenarios and outcomes. He had prepared for many contingencies, but the reality of their situation was more unpredictable than any plan could account for.

"I think we're as ready as we can be," Jamal said, looking at Keisha with a mixture of determination and apprehension. "We need to stay alert and be prepared for anything. Hartman's team is closing in, and we have to be one step ahead."

Keisha nodded, her expression resolute. "Agreed. We need to stick to the plan and be ready to adapt if things don't go as expected. I'll keep an eye on the surroundings while you finalize the last details."

They decided to take one last walk around the perimeter of the safe house, their senses heightened by the constant threat they faced. The forest, once a comforting escape, now felt like a potential trap. Every rustle of leaves and snap of twigs was analyzed for potential danger.

Around mid-morning, Jamal and Keisha received a call from Meat's driver. The news was both urgent and alarming. "Hartman's team has been spotted in the vicinity. They're conducting thorough searches and have increased their patrols. It's only a matter of time before they zero in on your location. You need to move now."

Jamal shared the news with Keisha, and the reality of their situation hit home. They had to act quickly, without the luxury of further preparation. They quickly gathered their belongings and made their way to the vehicle, their movements quick and precise. Every second counted, and they couldn't afford to waste any time.

As they loaded their supplies into the vehicle, Jamal's mind was racing. He had a general idea of their destination, but the specifics were still uncertain. They needed to find a safe location quickly, and the uncertainty of their situation made the task even more challenging.

Keisha drove while Jamal navigated, his eyes scanning the surroundings for any signs of danger. They had decided to head for a pre-determined safe house that had been suggested by Meat's driver. The location was remote and hidden, offering the best chance for temporary safety.

The drive was tense, each passing mile adding to their anxiety. Jamal and Keisha stayed alert, their eyes constantly searching for any signs of pursuit. The forested landscape blurred past them, a reminder of how isolated they had become. The feeling of being on the run was inescapable, and every twist and turn of the road seemed to amplify their sense of vulnerability.

As they approached their destination, Jamal's heart raced with anticipation. The safe house was located in a secluded area, far from the prying eyes of Hartman's team. The location was supposed to offer temporary refuge, but Jamal knew that it was only a stopgap solution. They needed to remain vigilant and continue their search for a more permanent solution.

When they arrived at the safe house, Jamal and Keisha quickly assessed the area. The location was hidden and well-protected, but they couldn't afford to let their guard down. They unloaded their supplies and conducted a thorough inspection of the property, ensuring that there were no immediate threats.

As they settled in, Jamal and Keisha took stock of their situation. The safe house was a temporary respite, but the threat from Hartman's team was still a constant concern. They knew that they had to remain vigilant and continue their search for a more permanent solution.

Later that evening, Jamal and Keisha gathered around a makeshift dining area, their exhaustion palpable. The safe house offered some comfort, but the constant tension made it difficult to relax. They took a moment to review their plans and discuss their next steps.

Jamal felt a growing sense of frustration. The constant movement and uncertainty were taking a toll, and he was eager to find a more stable solution. "We need to find a way to get ahead of Hartman's team. We can't keep running forever."

Keisha nodded in agreement. "I know. We need to come up with a plan to counter their efforts. Maybe there's a way to turn the tables and gain an advantage."

Jamal considered her words. "It's worth exploring. If we can find a way to disrupt their operations or create a diversion, it might give us the breathing room we need."

As they discussed their options, the reality of their situation continued to sink in. The safe house was a temporary refuge, but the challenges they faced were far from over. They knew that they had to remain resolute and continue their fight for safety and survival.

As night fell, Jamal and Keisha took their positions for the night watch. The quiet of the safe house was a stark contrast to the chaos of their lives, but it also served as a reminder of the ongoing danger. They knew that their fight was far from over, and they remained determined to navigate the challenges ahead with courage and resolve.

End of Chapter 17

Chapter 18: Shadows of the Past

The first light of dawn crept into the windows of the safe house, casting a soft glow over the room. Jamal and Keisha were already awake, their minds racing with the weight of their circumstances. The temporary respite provided by the safe house had not alleviated the constant tension—they knew that every moment of calm was a fleeting luxury.

Jamal sat at the small wooden table, his eyes scanning the maps and documents spread out before him. The papers were covered in notes and markings, a visual representation of their plans and contingencies. Despite his efforts to stay organized, the complexity of their situation made it difficult to find clarity. Hartman's team was relentless, and the ever-present threat was a constant drain on their resolve.

Keisha joined him at the table, her expression tired but determined. She had spent the early morning preparing breakfast, a small gesture of normalcy in the midst of their chaotic lives. "How's it looking?" she asked, taking a seat across from Jamal.

Jamal sighed, rubbing his temples. "It's hard to say. We're dealing with so many variables, and Hartman's team is making it even more complicated. We need to find a way to disrupt their operations or create some distance between us."

Keisha nodded, her gaze shifting to the metal casing they had set aside. "Have you had any luck with that thing?"

Jamal shook his head. "Not yet. It's still a mystery. I've tried to identify its components, but it's proving to be more complex than I anticipated. If we could figure out what it does, it might give us some insight into Hartman's plans."

After breakfast, Jamal and Keisha decided to take a closer look at their surroundings. The safe house was surrounded by dense forest, providing some level of isolation but also making it difficult to monitor the area effectively. They ventured outside to conduct a thorough inspection, their senses alert for any signs of danger.

As they walked through the woods, Jamal couldn't shake the feeling that they were being watched. The quiet of the forest was unsettling, each sound magnified by their heightened state of alert. They checked for any signs of recent activity or disturbances, hoping to ensure their safety.

During their inspection, they came across a small, hidden clearing. It was a serene spot, surrounded by tall trees and overgrown with foliage. The clearing seemed like a potential vantage point, offering a better view of their surroundings. Jamal and Keisha decided to use it as an observation post, setting up a makeshift watchtower to monitor the area.

As they worked on their new setup, Keisha's mind wandered back to their earlier discussions about creating a diversion. "Jamal, what if we could lure Hartman's team away from our location? We could use the resources we have to set up a false lead or create a diversion."

Jamal considered the idea. "It's worth a shot. If we can mislead them, it might buy us the time we need to regroup and plan our next move. But we need to be careful. If the diversion doesn't work, it could put us in an even worse position."

Keisha nodded in agreement. "We'll need to come up with a detailed plan and make sure it's executed perfectly. I'll start working on it, and we can review it together later."

The afternoon was spent devising their diversion strategy. Jamal and Keisha brainstormed ideas, drawing on their combined knowledge and resources. They discussed various tactics, including setting up false trails and creating misleading signals to throw off Hartman's team.

As they worked, Jamal couldn't help but reflect on their situation. The weight of their predicament was becoming increasingly burdensome, and the pressure was beginning to take a toll on him. He thought about their lives before all of this—the sense of normalcy and security that seemed so distant now.

Keisha, sensing his growing frustration, placed a reassuring hand on his shoulder. "We'll get through this, Jamal. We've faced challenges before, and we can face this one too. We just need to stay focused and keep moving forward."

Jamal appreciated her support. "You're right. We've come this far, and we can't give up now. We need to stay strong and keep pushing forward."

As evening approached, Jamal and Keisha finalized their plans and prepared for the execution of their diversion strategy. The safe house was still a temporary refuge, but they were determined to make the most of their opportunity.

Jamal and Keisha reviewed their roles and responsibilities, ensuring that each step of the plan was clearly understood. They discussed the timing and logistics, making sure that everything was in place for a successful diversion.

The execution of the plan began as night fell. Jamal and Keisha carefully set up their diversion, making sure that it was convincing enough to mislead Hartman's team. They placed misleading signals and created false trails, hoping to draw attention away from their actual location.

As they completed their preparations, they took a moment to review their progress. The diversion was set, and all they could do now was wait and hope that their efforts would be successful. The uncertainty of the situation weighed heavily on them, but they remained hopeful that their plan would provide the necessary relief.

Throughout the night, Jamal and Keisha maintained a vigilant watch. The safe house was quiet, the only sounds being the occasional rustle of leaves and the distant calls of wildlife. They remained alert, their senses attuned to any signs of movement or activity.

Around midnight, Jamal received a call from Meat's driver. The news was both promising and concerning. "We've heard reports that Hartman's team has been diverted by your efforts. They're following the false leads and seem to be moving away from your location. However, you need to stay vigilant. They might regroup and refocus their search."

Jamal relayed the news to Keisha, and they both felt a mix of relief and apprehension. Their diversion had been successful, but the threat was far from over. They knew that they needed to remain cautious and continue their preparations.

As the night wore on, Jamal and Keisha took turns monitoring the area, their exhaustion evident but their determination unwavering. The diversion had bought them some time, but the challenges they faced were far from over.

As the first light of dawn began to break, Jamal and Keisha felt a renewed sense of hope. Their diversion had provided a temporary respite, but they knew that they had to continue their fight for safety and survival. The path ahead was still fraught with challenges, but they were determined to navigate it with resilience and resolve.

The safe house had offered them a brief moment of calm, but the journey was far from over. Jamal and Keisha knew that they had to stay vigilant and prepared for whatever lay ahead. The fight for their safety and freedom was ongoing, and they were ready to face it with unwavering determination.

End of Chapter 18

Chapter 19: The Unraveling

The morning after the diversion was met with a cautious optimism. The temporary relief provided by their successful ruse was a welcome change from the constant tension they had endured. Jamal and Keisha knew, however, that this respite was not guaranteed to last. They had bought themselves time, but the threat from Hartman's team remained a looming concern.

Jamal and Keisha spent the early part of the day assessing their situation and planning their next steps. The safe house had provided them with a much-needed break, but the reality of their circumstances was ever-present. The quiet of the morning was a stark contrast to the chaos they had experienced, and it offered a brief but important opportunity to regroup and refocus.

Jamal sat at the table, reviewing the maps and documents they had collected. The information they had was extensive, but the complexity of their situation made it difficult to discern a clear path forward. He meticulously examined their escape routes and potential safe locations, trying to find a viable option for their next move.

Keisha, meanwhile, was busy with the logistics of their situation. She organized their supplies, ensuring that everything was in order and ready for their continued journey. She also took the time to review their communication devices, checking for any potential issues and making sure that they were fully operational.

By mid-morning, Jamal and Keisha decided to conduct another thorough inspection of their surroundings. The forest around the safe house offered some protection, but it also posed its own set of challenges. They needed to ensure that their new vantage point was secure and that there were no signs of unwanted visitors.

As they ventured into the forest, they remained vigilant. The serene beauty of the woods was a stark contrast to the danger they faced, and the feeling of being on high alert was a constant companion. They carefully examined the area around the clearing, looking for any signs of disturbance or recent activity.

During their inspection, Jamal noticed something unusual. The ground in a specific area seemed freshly disturbed, as if someone had recently been there. His heart raced as he considered the possibility that Hartman's team might have detected their diversion and was closing in on their location.

"Keisha, take a look at this," Jamal said, pointing to the disturbed ground. "It looks like someone's been here recently. We need to be extra cautious."

Keisha examined the area and nodded in agreement. "It's definitely worth investigating. We can't afford to take any chances."

They carefully examined the disturbed area, looking for any clues or signs of activity. The uncertainty of their situation was a constant burden, and every detail mattered. They needed to stay one step ahead of Hartman's team, and every potential threat had to be addressed.

Back at the safe house, Jamal and Keisha discussed their findings. The disturbed ground was a troubling sign, and they needed to determine if it was connected to their pursuers. They reviewed their plans and made adjustments based on the new information.

Jamal was frustrated. The constant shifting of their situation made it difficult to maintain a clear strategy. "We need to stay ahead of them. If they're getting closer, we need to have a backup plan ready."

Keisha agreed, her expression focused. "We should consider relocating to a new safe house. It's better to be proactive rather than waiting for them to find us."

Jamal nodded. "I think that's a good idea. We'll start looking for a new location and make sure that we're prepared to move quickly if necessary."

In the afternoon, Jamal and Keisha began their search for a new safe location. They used their maps and contacts to identify potential sites that offered a higher level of security. The search was meticulous, and they considered various factors, including accessibility, concealment, and proximity to potential resources.

As they worked on their search, Jamal received a call from Meat's driver. The driver's voice was tense and urgent. "We've received reports that Hartman's team has been on high alert. They're conducting searches in nearby areas, and it's possible that they're closing in on your location. You need to move quickly."

Jamal shared the news with Keisha, and they both felt a renewed sense of urgency. The threat from Hartman's team was becoming more immediate, and their time at the safe house was quickly running out. They needed to finalize their plans and prepare for a swift departure.

As evening approached, Jamal and Keisha made the final preparations for their move. They packed their supplies, double-checking that they had everything they needed. The sense of urgency was palpable, and they worked efficiently to ensure that they were ready for an immediate departure.

Jamal took one last look around the safe house, the weight of their situation pressing heavily on him. The safe house had been a temporary refuge, but the challenges they faced were far from over. He felt a growing frustration as they prepared to leave, knowing that their fight for safety and freedom was ongoing.

Keisha, sensing Jamal's frustration, offered words of encouragement. "We're doing everything we can, Jamal. We've faced challenges before, and we'll face this one too. We just need to stay focused and keep moving forward."

Jamal appreciated her support. "You're right. We've come this far, and we can't give up now. We need to stay strong and keep pushing forward."

As night fell, Jamal and Keisha set out for their new safe location. The drive was tense, each mile adding to their anxiety. The forested landscape was a constant reminder of their isolation, and the feeling of being on the run was inescapable.

They arrived at the new location, a secluded cabin nestled deep in the woods. The cabin was wellhidden and offered a higher level of security, but it was still a temporary solution. Jamal and Keisha quickly assessed the property, ensuring that it was safe and secure.

As they settled into their new safe house, Jamal and Keisha took a moment to review their situation.

The move had been necessary, but the threat from Hartman's team was still a constant concern. They knew that they had to remain vigilant and continue their preparations.

Jamal and Keisha took turns on watch, their exhaustion evident but their determination unwavering. The night was quiet, but the uncertainty of their situation made it difficult to relax. They knew that their fight for safety and freedom was far from over.

As the first light of dawn began to break, Jamal and Keisha felt a renewed sense of resolve. The new safe house offered them a brief moment of calm, but they knew that they had to stay vigilant and continue their fight. The path ahead was still fraught with challenges, but they were determined to navigate it with courage and resilience.

The safe house had provided them with a temporary respite, but the journey was far from over. Jamal and Keisha knew that they had to remain prepared for whatever lay ahead. The fight for their safety and freedom was ongoing, and they were ready to face it with unwavering determination.

End of Chapter 19

Chapter 20: Into the Abyss

The early morning light filtered through the narrow windows of the cabin, casting long shadows across the room. Jamal and Keisha had barely slept, their minds racing with the implications of their latest move. The new safe house was more secure than the previous one, but the constant threat from Hartman's team was an ever-present burden. The sense of urgency and fear hung in the air, making it nearly impossible to relax.

Jamal sat by the window, his eyes scanning the forest for any signs of activity. The tranquility of the forest was deceptive, hiding the danger that lurked just beyond. Keisha had prepared a simple breakfast, but the mood was subdued. Each bite was taken in silence, their thoughts preoccupied with the uncertainty of their situation.

As they ate, Keisha broke the silence. "Jamal, we need to think about what comes next. We've managed to stay ahead of Hartman's team so far, but we can't keep running forever. We need a long-term plan."

Jamal nodded, his expression serious. "You're right. We need to figure out a way to gain the upper hand. Maybe there's a way to get information on Hartman's operations or find a way to turn the tables."

Keisha considered this. "We've been relying on what we know and what we can deduce, but we might need more concrete information. If we can uncover more about Hartman's plans, it could give us an advantage."

Jamal agreed. "I've been thinking about that too. We need to find a way to gather intelligence or get some inside information. It might be risky, but it could be the key to turning this situation around."

The day was spent devising strategies and exploring potential options for gathering information. Jamal and Keisha used their limited resources to reach out to their contacts, hoping to find someone who could provide valuable intelligence about Hartman's operations.

Jamal made a series of phone calls, his voice calm but urgent as he spoke with various contacts. He inquired about any potential leads or sources of information, trying to piece together a clearer picture of Hartman's activities. Each conversation was a delicate balancing act, as they needed to gather information without drawing unwanted attention.

Keisha worked on the logistics of their plan, reviewing their resources and identifying potential risks. She considered the safest ways to gather information and ensure their continued safety. The cabin was a temporary refuge, and they needed to make the most of their time there.

As the afternoon wore on, Jamal received a promising lead from one of his contacts. "I've got some information for you. There's a local informant who might have insight into Hartman's operations. He's been known to deal in the same circles as Hartman's team. It could be worth checking out."

Jamal shared the news with Keisha, and they both felt a surge of hope. The informant could provide the crucial information they needed to gain an advantage. However, they also knew that approaching the informant would be risky and required careful planning.

In the evening, Jamal and Keisha began to prepare for their meeting with the informant. They made sure to take every precaution, understanding that the informant's safety and their own depended on discretion and careful planning. They reviewed their approach and ensured that they had everything they needed for a successful meeting.

Jamal was nervous but determined. The informant's information could be a turning point in their struggle against Hartman. He had to make sure that the meeting went smoothly and that they obtained the necessary intelligence.

Keisha, ever the meticulous planner, made final checks on their equipment and supplies. She reviewed their escape routes and contingency plans, ensuring that they were prepared for any eventuality. The safety of the meeting was paramount, and they needed to be ready for any unexpected developments.

As night fell, Jamal and Keisha set out for the meeting with the informant. The drive was tense, each passing mile adding to their anxiety. The forested roads were dark and secluded, and the sense of isolation was palpable.

When they arrived at the designated meeting location—a dimly lit, rundown diner on the outskirts of town—they were on high alert. The informant was known to be cautious and unpredictable, and Jamal and Keisha had to be prepared for anything.

They entered the diner and took a seat in a secluded booth. The informant, a wiry man with a shifty demeanor, arrived shortly after. He took a seat across from Jamal and Keisha, his eyes darting around nervously.

"Here's the deal," the informant said, his voice low. "I've got information on Hartman's operations. He's been moving a lot of product through a warehouse on the outskirts of town. There's a shipment coming in tonight, and it's expected to be heavily guarded."

Jamal's heart raced as he absorbed the information. "How reliable is this? And how do we use it to our advantage?"

The informant hesitated before answering. "It's pretty solid, but you need to be careful. Hartman's people are on high alert, and there's a lot of security. If you want to get in, you'll need to be smart about it."

Keisha asked, "Do you have any specific details about the warehouse's security or the shipment?"

The informant nodded. "I've heard there's a schedule for the guards and a list of security measures. I can get you that information, but it'll cost you."

Jamal and Keisha exchanged a glance. They needed the information, but they also had to manage their resources carefully. "How much?" Jamal asked.

The informant named a price that was steep but manageable. Jamal agreed, and the informant promised to provide the additional details within the next few hours.

Back at the cabin, Jamal and Keisha reviewed the information they had received. The details about the warehouse and the shipment were crucial, but they knew they had to approach the situation with caution. The security was extensive, and any misstep could jeopardize their safety.

They spent the night planning their next move, carefully analyzing the security measures and developing a strategy for infiltrating the warehouse. The information from the informant provided a clearer picture of the risks and opportunities.

As the night wore on, Jamal and Keisha finalized their plans and prepared for the next phase of their operation. They knew that the coming days would be critical, and they needed to be fully prepared for the challenges ahead.

In the early hours of the morning, Jamal and Keisha were ready to put their plan into action. They had spent the night preparing and were determined to make the most of the opportunity. The warehouse operation presented a potential breakthrough in their fight against Hartman, and they were prepared to take the risk.

The cabin had served its purpose as a temporary refuge, but the time had come to move forward. Jamal and Keisha were focused and resolute, their minds set on achieving their goals and staying one step ahead of their adversaries.

As they set out for the warehouse, the weight of their situation was heavy, but their determination was unwavering. The fight for their safety and freedom continued, and they were ready to face whatever lay ahead.

End of Chapter 20

Chapter 21: Into the Storm

The morning was gray and overcast, mirroring the tension that enveloped Jamal and Keisha as they prepared for their operation. The news from the informant had provided them with a crucial lead, but the risks involved were significant. They had spent the previous night meticulously planning their approach, but now the time had come to put their strategy into action.

Jamal and Keisha were already in the car, their equipment packed and ready. The journey to the warehouse was a delicate one; every mile was a step closer to the unknown, and every minute spent on the road increased their anxiety. The forested roads had a haunting quality in the early morning light, and the anticipation of what lay ahead was a constant undercurrent of tension.

The warehouse was located on the outskirts of town, nestled in an industrial area that was quiet during the early hours. Jamal and Keisha navigated the winding roads, their senses on high alert. The prospect of encountering Hartman's heavily guarded operation added a layer of urgency to their mission.

As they neared the warehouse, they took a moment to review their plan. Jamal was in charge of disabling the security systems, while Keisha was responsible for managing their entry and exit strategy. Both roles were critical, and the success of their operation depended on their ability to execute their plan flawlessly.

The warehouse loomed ahead, its exterior dimly lit and heavily fortified. Jamal and Keisha parked a safe distance away and began their approach on foot. The area around the warehouse was monitored by security cameras and patrolled by guards, and they had to navigate carefully to avoid detection.

They reached their vantage point—a small, concealed area near the side of the building. From here, they could observe the guards and the security systems in place. Jamal set up his equipment and began working on disabling the cameras and alarms. His hands were steady, but his mind was racing as he focused on the task at hand.

Keisha, meanwhile, was monitoring the guards' movements. She used a pair of binoculars to keep track of their patrol routes and identify any potential weaknesses in the security perimeter. Her observations were critical for ensuring that Jamal could work without interruption.

After several tense minutes, Jamal signaled that he had successfully disabled the cameras and alarms. They were ready to proceed. Keisha checked their gear one last time, making sure that everything was in place for their infiltration.

As they approached the main entrance of the warehouse, Jamal and Keisha encountered their first major obstacle: a heavy, reinforced door secured with an electronic lock. This was the final barrier between them and the valuable information they sought.

Jamal pulled out his tools and began working on the lock. It was a complex system, and he needed to be precise to avoid triggering any hidden alarms. Keisha kept a lookout, her eyes scanning the surroundings for any signs of activity.

The minutes ticked by slowly, each one amplifying the tension. Jamal's concentration was unwavering, his focus entirely on the lock mechanism. Finally, with a soft click, the door unlocked. Jamal gave Keisha a nod, and they slipped inside the warehouse.

Inside the warehouse, the atmosphere was dimly lit and filled with the faint hum of machinery. The layout was a maze of crates and equipment, and the air was thick with the scent of oil and metal. Jamal and Keisha moved cautiously, their footsteps muffled by the concrete floor.

They navigated through the warehouse, following the route they had planned. The informant's information had indicated that the shipment would be located in a specific section of the building. They needed to reach it quickly to gather the intelligence they required.

As they moved deeper into the warehouse, they encountered another security measure: a set of locked gates separating them from the shipment area. Jamal and Keisha assessed the situation and decided on a new approach. They would need to find a way around the gates or find another entrance to their target area.

They explored the surroundings, searching for an alternative route. Keisha spotted a maintenance tunnel that led beneath the warehouse, offering a potential way to bypass the gates. They made their way to the tunnel entrance, which was concealed behind a stack of crates.

The maintenance tunnel was narrow and dark, the only light coming from their flashlights. The tunnel system was extensive, and they had to navigate carefully to avoid getting lost. The air was damp and musty, adding to the oppressive atmosphere.

Jamal led the way, his flashlight casting eerie shadows on the tunnel walls. They followed the tunnel's twists and turns, their progress slow but steady. The path eventually led them to a service hatch that opened into the target area of the warehouse.

Keisha checked the area outside the hatch to ensure that it was clear. Once they were satisfied that it was safe, they climbed out and resumed their search for the shipment. The section of the warehouse they entered was filled with stacks of crates and barrels, each one marked with labels indicating its contents.

They found the shipment they were looking for: a large crate labeled with Hartman's emblem. The crate was heavily secured, and they needed to open it to access the contents. Jamal used his tools to carefully pry open the crate, revealing a trove of documents and equipment inside.

The documents were extensive, and Jamal and Keisha quickly began to sift through them. The papers contained valuable information about Hartman's operations, including details on upcoming shipments, security measures, and contacts within law enforcement.

As they worked, Keisha noticed something troubling. "Jamal, look at this. There's a list of names here—people who've been involved in Hartman's operations. Some of them are from the local police department."

Jamal examined the list, his face darkening with realization. "It looks like Hartman has a lot more influence than we thought. We need to be extremely careful. If any of these names are connected to Hartman's team, they could pose a serious threat."

With the documents secured, Jamal and Keisha prepared to leave the warehouse. They retraced their steps through the maintenance tunnel, their minds still processing the implications of the information they had uncovered.

As they emerged from the tunnel and made their way back to their car, they were on high alert. The warehouse operation had been a success, but the risks were still very real. They needed to ensure that they left no trace and that their escape was as discreet as their entry.

Back at the cabin, Jamal and Keisha reviewed the documents in detail. The information they had obtained was a significant breakthrough, but it also highlighted the complexity of the situation they faced. Hartman's connections within law enforcement added a new layer of danger to their struggle.

Jamal and Keisha knew that their fight was far from over. The information they had gathered would be crucial in their efforts to bring Hartman to justice, but they needed to remain vigilant and continue their preparations. The threat from Hartman's team was still a constant concern, and they had to be prepared for whatever came next.

As the night settled in, Jamal and Keisha took a moment to reflect on their progress. The warehouse operation had been a success, but it was just one step in a long and arduous journey. They were determined to see it through, no matter the challenges they faced.

The safe house had provided them with temporary refuge, but the fight for their safety and freedom continued. Jamal and Keisha were ready to face whatever lay ahead, their resolve strengthened by the knowledge that they were one step closer to achieving their goals.

End of Chapter 21

Chapter 22: Tides of Change

The dawn broke with an eerie calm as Jamal and Keisha awoke to a new day. The information they had retrieved from the warehouse was a game-changer, but the implications of their discovery were both exciting and daunting. The documents revealed Hartman's extensive network and the dangerous depths of his corruption, but they also underscored the gravity of their predicament. The weight of their new knowledge settled heavily on their shoulders.

They began their day with a strategic review. The documents were spread out across the table, each page a piece of the puzzle they needed to solve. Jamal and Keisha went through the material methodically, extracting key information and assessing how best to use it. The documents contained details about Hartman's various operations, including a series of illicit transactions and communication logs that could potentially expose his network.

"Look at this," Jamal said, pointing to a series of entries in a ledger. "These are detailed records of shipments, including dates, quantities, and even the names of people involved. This could give us a clearer picture of how Hartman's operation is structured."

Keisha nodded in agreement. "This information is gold. If we can use it to connect the dots and find out who's been helping Hartman, we might be able to leverage it to our advantage."

Jamal continued, "We also need to consider how to handle this information. If we just release it without context, it might not have the impact we need. We should think about our next steps carefully."

Keisha agreed. "We should find a way to get this information to the right people—those who can use it to take Hartman down. But we also need to stay cautious. If Hartman's network is as extensive as it looks, he might have eyes and ears everywhere."

The day was spent planning their next move. They needed to balance the need for action with the necessity of caution. Jamal and

Keisha discussed their options, considering various strategies for using the information to expose Hartman's network while ensuring their own safety.

As part of their strategy, Jamal reached out to trusted contacts who might help disseminate the information securely. He contacted a few investigative journalists known for their integrity and commitment to uncovering the truth. It was crucial to ensure that the information reached people who could handle it responsibly and with the necessary discretion.

Meanwhile, Keisha focused on fortifying their current location. They had been fortunate so far, but they knew that the threat from Hartman's team was still a significant risk. Keisha took inventory of their supplies, double-checked their security measures, and made sure that they had everything they needed for a quick departure if necessary.

As evening approached, Jamal received a response from one of the journalists he had contacted. The journalist expressed interest in the information and agreed to meet in person to discuss the details. Jamal arranged for a secure meeting location, a quiet, nondescript café on the edge of town.

Jamal and Keisha prepared for the meeting with the journalist. They gathered the most pertinent documents and made sure to conceal their identities to protect themselves from potential fallout. They arrived at the café early, taking a seat at a corner table where they could observe the surroundings.

The journalist arrived promptly, a middle-aged woman with a keen, analytical gaze. She introduced herself as Karen and took a seat across from Jamal and Keisha. The conversation was conducted in hushed tones, the atmosphere tense with anticipation.

Karen listened intently as Jamal and Keisha explained the details of the information they had uncovered. She took notes and asked probing questions, her demeanor professional but focused. The weight of the documents was evident, and Karen's experience in investigative journalism gave Jamal and Keisha confidence that their information would be handled appropriately.

As they discussed the details, Karen made several key observations. "The scope of this operation is extensive. It will take time to verify the information and connect the dots, but if what you've provided is accurate, it could be a major breakthrough."

Jamal and Keisha agreed. "We've done our best to ensure the accuracy of the information, but we're relying on you to take it from here. We need to remain low-profile and avoid drawing attention."

Karen nodded. "I understand. I'll start working on this immediately and keep you updated. In the meantime, make sure to stay safe. Hartman's network is likely to be watching closely."

After the meeting, Jamal and Keisha returned to the cabin with a renewed sense of hope. They had taken a significant step toward exposing Hartman's operations, but the road ahead was still fraught with challenges. The information they had provided was just the beginning; the next phase of their plan involved monitoring developments and preparing for potential retaliation.

The night was filled with anxious anticipation. Jamal and Keisha reviewed their plans and made final adjustments, ensuring that they were ready for any eventuality. The threat from Hartman's team remained a constant concern, and they needed to be prepared for any countermeasures.

As they settled into their routine, Jamal and Keisha received updates from Karen over the next few days. The investigation was progressing, and the journalist had made significant headway in verifying the information and connecting the various pieces of the puzzle. The exposure of Hartman's network was starting to take shape, and the implications were far-reaching.

The days that followed were a whirlwind of activity. Jamal and Keisha continued to monitor the situation closely, staying in constant communication with Karen. They remained vigilant, knowing that Hartman's network would not take kindly to their interference.

One evening, as they were preparing dinner, Keisha received a call from Karen. "Jamal, Keisha, I've got some important news. We've managed to verify much of the information you provided, and it's going to make headlines soon. Hartman's operations are being exposed, and the fallout is starting."

Jamal's heart raced with a mix of relief and anxiety. "That's great news. But what about the potential backlash? What should we expect?"

Karen's voice was serious. "Hartman's network is already mobilizing. You need to be extra cautious. I recommend taking additional security measures and being prepared for anything."

The news of Hartman's exposure was a significant victory, but it also marked a new phase in Jamal and Keisha's struggle. They knew that their fight was far from over and that the dangers they faced were likely to intensify.

As they prepared for the next steps, Jamal and Keisha reflected on their journey. They had faced numerous challenges and obstacles, but their determination and resilience had brought them this far. The road ahead would be difficult, but they were ready to confront whatever lay ahead.

The cabin, once a sanctuary, now felt like a temporary haven in the midst of a storm. Jamal and Keisha knew that they needed to stay focused and continue their fight for justice. Their resolve was unwavering, and they were prepared to face the challenges that awaited them.

The battle against Hartman's network was far from over, but Jamal and Keisha were determined to see it through. They had made significant progress, and their efforts were beginning to yield results. The fight for their safety and for justice continued, and they were ready to face the storm head-on.

End of Chapter 22

Chapter 23: Shadows and Echoes

The aftermath of the information leak began to unfold rapidly. The media coverage was intense, with headlines blaring about Hartman's corruption and illicit activities. The exposure was causing a ripple effect throughout the community, and the political landscape was shifting. As the revelations spread, Jamal and Keisha felt the increasing pressure of their situation.

The cabin, which had once been a secure hiding place, now felt like a ticking clock. The tension in the air was palpable as they awaited the fallout from the exposure. The warehouse documents had set a chain of events into motion, and Jamal and Keisha were bracing themselves for the potential repercussions.

The morning after the media frenzy began, Jamal and Keisha watched the news from a small, outdated television they had in the cabin. The broadcast was dominated by reports of Hartman's exposure and the ongoing investigation. The coverage included interviews with local officials, law enforcement, and citizens reacting to the scandal.

"This is really blowing up," Keisha remarked, her eyes fixed on the screen. "Hartman's empire is unraveling faster than we anticipated."

Jamal nodded, his face grim. "It's good that the information is out there, but we need to stay alert. Hartman's not going to just sit back and let this happen. He'll retaliate."

They both knew that the fallout from the exposure would likely bring increased danger. Hartman's network was vast and well-connected, and the risk of retaliation was high. They needed to be prepared for any potential threats.

As the day wore on, Jamal and Keisha received word from Karen. The journalist was making significant progress in her investigation, and the evidence was piling up. However, Karen also warned them about increased activity from Hartman's associates.

"I've received some disturbing information," Karen said over the phone. "Hartman's people are on high alert. They're conducting sweeps and looking for anyone who might have had contact with the leaked information. You need to be extra cautious."

Jamal's heart sank. "What are the chances they'll trace the information back to us?"

Karen's voice was steady but concerned. "There's a possibility. They're trying to cover all bases. I recommend that you change your location and be prepared for anything."

That evening, Jamal and Keisha packed their essentials and prepared to leave the cabin. They had made arrangements for a new safe house through a contact they trusted, and they were ready to move on short notice. The sense of urgency was heightened by the threat of Hartman's retaliation.

As they loaded their car, Keisha checked their security measures one last time. "We need to make sure we're not being followed. It's crucial to stay under the radar."

Jamal agreed. "I'll take the lead and check the area before we leave. We can't afford any mistakes."

Jamal conducted a thorough sweep of the area around the cabin, looking for any signs of surveillance or unusual activity. The forest surrounding the cabin was dense and quiet, but Jamal knew that appearances could be deceiving. After a careful inspection, he determined that the area was clear and gave the signal to proceed.

The drive to the new safe house was tense and uneventful. Jamal and Keisha stayed alert, their eyes scanning the roads and surroundings for any signs of being followed. The journey took them through a series of winding roads and backcountry routes, minimizing the chance of detection.

When they arrived at the new location, they were greeted by a trusted contact who had prepared the safe house for them. The house was secluded and well-equipped, providing a new sense of security. Jamal and Keisha settled in and began to get familiar with their new surroundings.

The new safe house was a marked improvement in terms of security. It was equipped with surveillance cameras, reinforced doors, and an elaborate alarm system. The isolation of the location also offered a sense of respite from the constant danger.

Jamal and Keisha wasted no time in setting up their operations. They established communication channels with Karen and reviewed any new developments in the ongoing investigation. The documents they had provided were still making waves, and the investigation was uncovering more connections and implicating additional figures in the corruption scandal.

As the days passed, Jamal and Keisha continued to monitor the situation. They stayed in close contact with Karen, who provided regular updates on the progress of the investigation. The exposure of Hartman's network was having a profound impact, but the danger was far from over.

One afternoon, as they were reviewing new information, Keisha received an unexpected call. It was one of their old contacts from the underground network they had previously engaged with. The contact, known as Rick, was someone Jamal and Keisha had trusted for years.

"Jamal, Keisha, it's Rick. I've been keeping an eye on things from my end, and I've got some intel that you might find useful," Rick said, his voice low and urgent.

Jamal's interest was piqued. "What do you have for us?"

Rick continued, "Hartman's associates are planning a major move. They're attempting to consolidate their resources and potentially target anyone who's been involved in exposing them. I've got a list of their planned operations and key players. It might give you an edge."

Keisha took notes as Rick detailed the information. "This is valuable. We need to figure out how to use it to stay ahead and protect ourselves."

Rick agreed. "I'll keep monitoring and provide updates as I can. Just stay safe out there. It's a dangerous time."

As they processed the new intelligence, Jamal and Keisha realized that Hartman's network was more dangerous and resourceful than they had anticipated. The consolidation of resources and planned operations posed a serious threat, and they needed to adapt their strategy accordingly.

They spent the next few days refining their plans, focusing on ways to stay ahead of Hartman's associates and avoid becoming targets. They also continued to follow up with Karen and Rick, integrating the new information into their strategy.

The safe house provided a temporary refuge, but Jamal and Keisha knew that their fight was far from over. They were determined to see their efforts through to the end, no matter the risks involved. The exposure of Hartman's corruption was just one part of a larger battle, and they were prepared to confront whatever challenges lay ahead.

As the days turned into weeks, the impact of the investigation continued to unfold. The community was abuzz with discussions about the scandal, and the political landscape was shifting as more figures were implicated. Jamal and Keisha remained vigilant, knowing that the danger was everpresent.

One evening, as they reviewed the latest updates, Jamal received a call from Karen. "I've got some significant news," Karen said. "The investigation has reached a critical point. There's a major development that could change everything."

Jamal's heart raced. "What's the news?"

Karen's voice was filled with anticipation. "We've managed to secure enough evidence to implicate several key figures in Hartman's network. There's a planned operation to arrest them, and it's happening soon. This could be a major breakthrough."

The news was a beacon of hope, but Jamal and Keisha knew that they needed to stay cautious. The arrest operation could trigger a final push from Hartman's associates, and they had to be prepared for any potential retaliation.

As they continued to plan and prepare, Jamal and Keisha remained focused on their goals. The fight against Hartman's network was nearing a critical juncture, and they were determined to see it through to the end.

The journey had been arduous and fraught with danger, but Jamal and Keisha's resolve was unwavering. They were ready to face the final challenges and continue their fight for justice, no matter the risks involved.

End of Chapter 23

Chapter 24: Crossroads and Confrontations

The days following Karen's call were a whirlwind of anticipation and anxiety. Jamal and Keisha were acutely aware that the endgame of their fight against Hartman's network was approaching, but the uncertainty of what lay ahead made every moment tense. The investigation had reached a critical point, and the imminent arrest operation was a turning point that could either dismantle Hartman's empire or escalate the danger to new heights.

The safe house, though secure and well-equipped, now felt like a temporary shell in the midst of a brewing storm. Jamal and Keisha had grown accustomed to the constant vigilance, but the reality of their situation was starting to weigh heavily on them. They knew that the arrest operation would bring a new wave of threats and that their role in the unfolding drama was far from over.

One evening, as they were reviewing the latest updates from Karen, Keisha's phone buzzed with an incoming call. The caller ID displayed an unknown number. With a glance at Jamal, Keisha answered the call, her voice cautious.

"Hello?"

A gruff voice on the other end responded. "Keisha, it's Rick. We've got a problem."

Jamal's attention immediately focused on the conversation. "What's going on, Rick?"

Rick's voice was urgent. "I've just heard that Hartman's associates have been ramping up their efforts. They're making a final push to secure their remaining operations and are targeting anyone involved in the investigation. They might be coming after you." Keisha's grip tightened on the phone. "How serious is the threat?"

Rick replied, "From what I'm hearing, it's serious. They're planning coordinated strikes to eliminate anyone who's been a thorn in their side. You need to stay on high alert."

Jamal took over the conversation. "Thanks for the heads-up, Rick. We'll take precautions. Keep us informed if you hear anything else."

Rick agreed. "I will. Stay safe and be careful."

As the phone call ended, Jamal and Keisha exchanged concerned looks. The new information from Rick confirmed their fears: Hartman's network was preparing for a final showdown. The arrest operation, while promising, had triggered a heightened level of danger.

"We need to fortify our position," Jamal said, pacing the room. "We can't afford to be caught off guard."

Keisha nodded in agreement. "We should review our security measures again and make sure we're prepared for any eventuality."

They spent the next few hours going over their security protocols, reinforcing the safe house's defenses, and preparing emergency plans. They also reviewed the latest intelligence from Karen, focusing on the specifics of the planned arrest operation.

The arrest operation was scheduled for the following week, and the coordination involved was intricate. Karen provided detailed information about the timing and target locations, and Jamal and Keisha used this to anticipate potential fallout and threats.

As the day of the operation approached, Jamal and Keisha remained on high alert. They kept in close contact with Karen, who provided updates on the progress of the investigation and any new developments. The anticipation was building, and the atmosphere was charged with a mix of hope and anxiety.

On the day of the operation, Jamal and Keisha decided to stay in close proximity to their safe house but maintained a low profile. They monitored the news and any developments related to the arrests, waiting for confirmation that the operation had been successfully carried out.

The news reports began to filter in as the day progressed. The operation had indeed commenced, and there were reports of several high-profile arrests related to Hartman's network. The news was met with a mix of relief and apprehension.

"We're getting reports of significant progress," Keisha said, watching the news coverage. "It looks like the operation is going well."

Jamal, however, remained cautious. "We still need to be careful. Hartman's associates won't take this lying down. They'll likely try to retaliate."

As the evening approached, Karen called with an update. "The operation has been largely successful. Many of Hartman's key associates have been arrested, and the network is being dismantled. But there are still some loose ends. We're expecting a final push from their side."

Jamal's mind raced. "What do we need to do to stay safe?"

Karen replied, "Maintain your current precautions and be prepared for any potential threats. If you need to relocate again, have a plan in place."

Jamal and Keisha acknowledged the advice and prepared for any eventuality. They reviewed their emergency protocols once more and ensured that they were ready to act quickly if needed.

The night passed with a tense quiet. Jamal and Keisha remained vigilant, constantly monitoring the news and any developments related to Hartman's network. The anticipation of potential retaliation kept them on edge, but they were determined to stay one step ahead.

As the days continued, the fallout from the operation became increasingly apparent. The arrests had sent shockwaves through the community, and the political landscape was shifting as a result. The investigation had revealed the extent of Hartman's corruption, and the impact was being felt far beyond what Jamal and Keisha had anticipated.

The media continued to cover the story, with new revelations and updates emerging regularly. Jamal and Keisha were relieved to see that their efforts had contributed to a significant breakthrough, but they knew that the danger was not yet over.

One afternoon, as Jamal and Keisha were reviewing the latest news reports, they received another call from Karen. Her voice was a mix of exhaustion and relief.

"The investigation has made considerable progress," Karen said. "The remaining elements of Hartman's network are being targeted, and the authorities are moving quickly. It looks like we're approaching the final stages."

Jamal felt a surge of relief. "That's good news. What should we expect in the coming days?"

Karen replied, "There will likely be some residual activity from Hartman's associates, but the bulk of their operations have been dismantled. You should remain cautious but start considering your next steps."

With the endgame in sight, Jamal and Keisha began to reflect on their journey. The fight against Hartman's network had been arduous, and they had faced numerous challenges along the way. The exposure of the corruption and the ongoing investigation had been a testament to their resilience and determination.

As they prepared for the final stages of their journey, Jamal and Keisha took stock of their accomplishments and considered their future. They had achieved a significant victory, but the road ahead remained uncertain. They knew that they needed to stay vigilant and continue their fight for justice, no matter the challenges that lay ahead.

The safe house, once a temporary refuge, now felt like a symbol of their journey—a place of both safety and uncertainty. Jamal and Keisha were ready to face whatever came next, knowing that their efforts had made a difference and that their fight was far from over.

End of Chapter 24

Chapter 25: The Calm Before the Storm

With the endgame approaching, Jamal and Keisha found themselves in a precarious situation. The dismantling of Hartman's network was drawing near, but the final stages of the operation were fraught with uncertainty. Their safe house, though secure, had become a constant reminder of the dangers they faced. The quiet days were punctuated by moments of intense activity as they prepared for potential threats and monitored the unfolding events.

The media coverage continued to evolve, with new reports and developments emerging daily. The arrest of key figures in Hartman's network was a significant achievement, but the fallout from the operation was still unfolding. Jamal and Keisha stayed tuned to the news, watching for any signs of retaliation or new threats.

One morning, as they sipped their coffee and reviewed the latest news, Keisha's phone buzzed with an incoming call. The caller ID displayed Karen's number. Jamal's attention immediately shifted to the conversation.

"Hello, Karen," Keisha said, her voice steady.

Karen's voice was filled with urgency. "Keisha, Jamal, we have a situation. Hartman's associates are planning a major counterstrike. They're targeting key locations involved in the investigation and potentially anyone connected to it."

Jamal's heart raced. "What kind of counterstrike?"

Karen explained, "They're mobilizing a coordinated effort to disrupt the ongoing operations and potentially retaliate against those who exposed them. It's crucial that you stay alert and be prepared for anything."

Keisha's face grew serious. "What should we do?"

Karen replied, "You need to enhance your security measures and be ready to relocate if necessary. I'm working on additional intel and will keep you updated."

After the call, Jamal and Keisha immediately sprang into action. They reviewed their security protocols, ensuring that all measures were up to date. The threat from Hartman's associates had intensified, and they needed to be prepared for any potential attacks.

Jamal checked their surveillance systems and made sure that all security measures were functioning properly. Keisha reviewed their emergency plans, updating them to account for the new threat. They also made arrangements for a quick evacuation if needed.

"We need to stay ahead of them," Jamal said, his voice determined. "Let's make sure we're prepared for every possible scenario."

Keisha agreed. "We've come this far, and we can't afford to be caught off guard now."

As the day progressed, Jamal and Keisha received additional updates from Karen. The counterstrike was taking shape, with reports of increased activity from Hartman's associates. The authorities were ramping up their efforts to protect key locations and personnel, but the situation remained volatile.

In the evening, Jamal and Keisha reviewed their preparations once more. They had packed their essentials and made arrangements for a new safe location, just in case they needed to relocate quickly. The tension in the air was palpable as they waited for further updates.

As they prepared dinner, Keisha reflected on their journey. "It's been a long road, Jamal. We've faced so many challenges, but we're almost at the finish line."

Jamal nodded. "It's been tough, but we've come through it together. We just need to stay focused and finish what we started."

The night was filled with a tense quiet as Jamal and Keisha settled in for what they hoped would be a relatively calm evening. The threat from Hartman's associates was still looming, but they were determined to remain vigilant.

In the early hours of the morning, Jamal was jolted awake by a sudden noise. He immediately sprang into action, his senses on high alert. Keisha, equally alert, joined him as they quickly assessed the situation.

The noise turned out to be a minor disturbance—a fallen branch outside the safe house. Despite the false alarm, Jamal and Keisha remained on edge, knowing that the danger was still very real.

The following day, Karen called with a critical update. "The counterstrike from Hartman's associates has begun. There are reports of targeted attacks on key locations, and the situation is escalating. You need to be extra cautious."

Jamal's face grew serious. "What are the authorities doing to address the situation?"

Karen replied, "They're deploying additional resources to protect the targeted locations and respond to the attacks. However, there's still a risk of collateral damage. It's important that you remain prepared for any eventuality."

Jamal and Keisha took Karen's advice to heart. They reviewed their plans once more, ensuring that they were ready for any potential threats. The safe house provided a temporary refuge, but they knew that their safety was not guaranteed.

As the day continued, the news reports began to reflect the escalating situation. There were reports of attacks on key locations related to the investigation, and the authorities were working to contain the damage. The situation was fluid, and the threat of further attacks was ever-present.

Jamal and Keisha stayed in close contact with Karen, receiving updates on the situation and any new developments. They remained vigilant, knowing that the final stages of the operation were the most critical.

In the evening, Jamal and Keisha decided to take a brief break from their preparations. They went for a walk around the property, taking a moment to clear their minds and reflect on their journey. The secluded surroundings provided a temporary escape from the tension of the situation.

As they walked, Keisha took a deep breath and spoke. "It's strange to think about how much has changed in such a short time. We started out trying to make a difference, and now we're in the middle of a major operation."

Jamal nodded. "It's been a wild ride, but we've made a real impact. We just need to see it through to the end."

As night fell, Jamal and Keisha returned to the safe house and continued their preparations. The threat from Hartman's associates remained a constant concern, but they were determined to stay ahead of the danger.

The calm before the storm was a brief reprieve, and Jamal and Keisha knew that the coming days would be critical. They were prepared for the final stages of their fight, and they were ready to confront whatever challenges lay ahead.

Their journey had been marked by danger and uncertainty, but they had persevered. The exposure of Hartman's network was a significant achievement, but the fight for justice was far from over.

As they settled in for the night, Jamal and Keisha remained vigilant, knowing that their efforts had made a difference and that their fight was nearing its final stages. The road ahead was uncertain, but they were prepared to face whatever came next.

End of Chapter 25

Chapter 26: Echoes of Retribution

The quietude of the safe house belied the chaos that was unfolding outside. As the arrest operation and Hartman's associates' counterstrikes continued, Jamal and Keisha found themselves caught in a maelstrom of uncertainty and anticipation. The coming days were crucial, and they knew that their every move needed to be calculated and precise.

The morning began with a sense of foreboding. Jamal and Keisha had barely slept through the night, their minds racing with the potential repercussions of the escalating situation. They had remained on high alert, monitoring news updates and coordinating with Karen, who had been their lifeline throughout the ordeal.

Jamal was pacing the room, his thoughts consumed by the recent developments. "We need to make sure we're not only prepared for the immediate threats but also for any longer-term consequences. Hartman's network may still have some resources at their disposal."

Keisha was seated at the table, her laptop open as she reviewed the latest intelligence. "I've been tracking the reports of attacks and disruptions. The authorities are doing their best to contain the damage, but there's a lot of chaos right now."

As they spoke, Keisha's phone rang. It was Karen, her voice tense and urgent. "Jamal, Keisha, we have a critical update. Hartman's associates have launched a coordinated effort to target key figures involved in the investigation. They're focusing on individuals who were instrumental in exposing the corruption."

Jamal's heart raced. "Who's at risk?"

Karen replied, "The authorities have already deployed additional security for the key figures, but there's still a risk. You should be extra cautious and be prepared for any potential threats."

With the new information, Jamal and Keisha reinforced their security measures. They conducted a thorough sweep of the safe house, ensuring that all security systems were functioning correctly. They also reviewed their emergency plans, making sure they were ready to evacuate quickly if needed.

The tension in the air was palpable as they prepared for the worst. Jamal knew that the threat was not just from Hartman's associates but also from the unpredictable nature of the situation. The chaos outside made it difficult to discern the true extent of the danger.

As the day wore on, the media coverage continued to evolve. There were reports of increasing violence and unrest, with Hartman's associates launching attacks on key locations. The authorities were working tirelessly to manage the situation, but the chaos was overwhelming.

Jamal and Keisha stayed in constant communication with Karen, who provided updates on the unfolding events. They were also receiving information from their network of contacts, who were keeping an eye on the situation from various vantage points.

In the late afternoon, Jamal received a call from Rick. "Jamal, Keisha, I've got some important information. Hartman's associates are planning a major move tonight. They're targeting a highprofile event where several key figures will be present."

Jamal's eyes widened. "What kind of move?"

Rick replied, "It's hard to say for sure, but there's a possibility of a significant attack. You need to be especially cautious and be prepared to take action if necessary."

Keisha looked at Jamal with concern. "We need to consider relocating again. If Hartman's associates are planning something major, we could be in immediate danger."

Jamal nodded in agreement. "Let's get our emergency plans in order and be ready to move if we need to."

The evening was marked by a heightened sense of urgency. Jamal and Keisha packed their essentials and prepared for a potential evacuation. They reviewed their plans, ensuring that they had everything they needed and that they could execute their plans swiftly if required.

As they prepared, they received another update from Karen. "The situation is becoming increasingly volatile. The authorities are focusing on the high-profile event, but there's still a risk of collateral damage. Stay on high alert and be prepared for any eventuality."

Jamal's face was grim. "We're ready. We'll continue to monitor the situation and act accordingly."

As night fell, Jamal and Keisha kept a close watch on the news and any developments related to the high-profile event. The tension was palpable as they waited for updates, their minds racing with the potential outcomes.

The news reports began to reflect the escalating situation. There were reports of increased security measures at the event, but the threat of an attack remained high. The authorities were working to contain the danger, but the uncertainty of the situation made it difficult to predict what would happen next.

Jamal and Keisha stayed vigilant, knowing that the coming hours would be critical. They remained on standby, ready to take action if necessary.

In the early hours of the morning, the situation reached a crescendo. There were reports of a major incident at the high-profile event, with several key figures involved in the investigation being targeted. The news was filled with images of chaos and confusion, and the authorities were working to manage the aftermath.

Jamal and Keisha were on edge, awaiting confirmation of the details. Karen called with an update. "The situation is intense. There have been significant disruptions, and several key figures have been affected. The authorities are doing their best to contain the damage."

Jamal's voice was tense. "What does this mean for us?"

Karen replied, "The immediate danger may have passed, but the situation is still fluid. You need to stay cautious and be prepared for any further developments."

As the day began, the fallout from the incident was still unfolding. The media coverage was dominated by reports of the attack, and the authorities were working to assess the full extent of the damage. The chaos from the previous night had set the stage for further uncertainty.

Jamal and Keisha continued to monitor the news and any new developments. They remained in contact with Karen and their network of contacts, gathering information and preparing for any potential threats.

The safe house, once a symbol of refuge, now felt like a temporary shelter in the midst of a storm. Jamal and Keisha knew that their fight was nearing its final stages, but the dangers they faced were still very real.

In the evening, Jamal and Keisha reflected on their journey. The exposure of Hartman's network and the subsequent fallout had been a significant achievement, but the road ahead remained uncertain. They had faced numerous challenges and threats, and their efforts had made a real impact.

As they prepared for the final stages of their journey, Jamal and Keisha remained focused on their goals. The fight for justice was not over, and they were determined to see it through to the end.

The calm before the storm had given way to a new phase of their battle. The dangers they faced were heightened, but their resolve was unwavering. Jamal and Keisha were ready to confront whatever came next, knowing that their efforts had made a difference and that their fight was far from over.

End of Chapter 26

Chapter 27: Shadows of Justice

The early morning light brought a momentary calm to the chaotic world outside the safe house. Jamal and Keisha had spent a sleepless night, their minds racing with the ramifications of the previous day's events. The attack at the high-profile event had sent shockwaves through the community, and the aftermath was still unfolding. The authorities were scrambling to manage the damage, and the news was filled with images of chaos and confusion.

In the quiet of the morning, Jamal and Keisha gathered in the kitchen, their faces etched with exhaustion and determination. They had been on high alert for days, and the weight of the situation was beginning to take its toll. The safe house, once a sanctuary, now felt like a pressure cooker of tension and uncertainty.

Keisha sipped her coffee, her eyes focused on the laptop in front of her. "The news reports are still coming in. The authorities are trying to piece together what happened at the event, but it's clear that the situation is far from resolved."

Jamal nodded, rubbing his temples. "We need to stay on top of this. If Hartman's associates are still out there, we could be in danger. We can't afford to let our guard down."

As they discussed their next steps, Jamal's phone buzzed with a new message. It was from Karen, her tone serious. "We've got new information. There are reports of a planned retaliation against those who were involved in the investigation. You need to be prepared for any potential threats."

Jamal shared the message with Keisha, and they both felt a renewed sense of urgency. The threat of retaliation added a new layer of danger to their already precarious situation.

Throughout the day, Jamal and Keisha continued to monitor the news and stay in touch with Karen. The authorities had intensified their efforts to protect key figures and prevent further attacks, but the uncertainty of the situation made it difficult to predict what would happen next.

Jamal decided it was time to review their plans once more. "We need to be ready for anything. The threat of retaliation means we have to be proactive. Let's go over our emergency protocols and ensure that everything is in place."

Keisha agreed, and they spent the afternoon reviewing their plans, making sure that they had everything they needed and that they could execute their plans quickly if necessary. They also took the time to review the latest intelligence from Karen, focusing on any new developments that could impact their safety.

As the day turned into evening, the atmosphere was thick with tension. Jamal and Keisha were on edge, knowing that the threat from Hartman's associates was still very real. They had fortified their safe house and prepared for any potential threats, but the danger was ever-present.

In the early evening, Karen called with a critical update. "The authorities have identified several potential targets for retaliation. They're increasing security at these locations, but there's still a risk. You need to stay vigilant and be prepared for any further developments."

Jamal's face was grim. "We'll stay on high alert. Is there any additional information on where the threats might be coming from?"

Karen replied, "The intelligence is still coming in, but it's clear that Hartman's associates are planning a significant move. Stay in contact with your network and keep me informed of any changes in your situation."

As night fell, Jamal and Keisha continued to monitor the situation. The news reports were filled with updates on the ongoing investigation and the authorities' efforts to contain the fallout from the attack. The media coverage was extensive, and the situation remained fluid.

Jamal and Keisha took turns keeping watch, their eyes scanning the news and any developments related to Hartman's associates. The tension in the safe house was palpable, and they remained ready to act at a moment's notice.

In the late hours of the night, Jamal received a call from Rick. "Jamal, Keisha, I've got some important information. There are reports of increased activity from Hartman's associates in a nearby area. They might be planning something significant."

Jamal's heart raced. "What kind of activity?"

Rick replied, "It's unclear at the moment, but it's enough to warrant concern. You should be extra cautious and be prepared to relocate if necessary."

Keisha looked at Jamal with concern. "We need to make sure we're ready for any potential threats. If Hartman's associates are planning something nearby, we could be in immediate danger."

Jamal nodded in agreement. "Let's review our evacuation plans and ensure that we can move quickly if we need to."

The early morning hours were filled with a sense of urgency as Jamal and Keisha reviewed their plans once more. The threat from Hartman's associates was growing, and they needed to be prepared for any eventuality. They packed their essentials and made sure that they were ready to evacuate quickly if necessary.

As they prepared, Keisha took a moment to reflect. "It's been a long and challenging journey, but we're close to the end. We just need to stay focused and see this through."

Jamal agreed. "We've come too far to back down now. We need to stay vigilant and continue our fight for justice."

The day dawned with a new set of challenges. The news continued to report on the ongoing situation, with updates on the authorities' efforts to manage the fallout from the attack. Jamal and Keisha remained on high alert, knowing that the danger was far from over.

Karen called with an update. "The authorities have identified several new threats and are taking additional measures to protect key figures. The situation is still volatile, but they're making progress."

Jamal's face was determined. "We'll continue to stay vigilant and be prepared for any potential threats. We're ready to act if necessary."

As the day continued, Jamal and Keisha maintained their vigilance. They monitored the news, stayed in touch with Karen, and prepared for any potential threats. The safe house provided a temporary refuge, but the dangers outside were very real.

The afternoon brought a brief respite as Jamal and Keisha took a moment to regroup. They reviewed their achievements and reflected on their journey. The exposure of Hartman's network and the ongoing investigation had been a significant accomplishment, but the fight for justice was not yet complete.

Jamal and Keisha knew that they needed to stay focused and see their efforts through to the end. The threat from Hartman's associates was a reminder of the challenges they faced, but it also fueled their determination.

As the day turned into evening, the news reports continued to cover the unfolding situation. The authorities were working tirelessly to manage the aftermath of the attack, and the media coverage was extensive.

Jamal and Keisha remained on high alert, ready to respond to any new developments. The final stages of their journey were approaching, and they were prepared to confront whatever came next.

In the quiet moments of the evening, Jamal and Keisha took stock of their situation. The safe house had become a symbol of their struggle—a place of refuge and uncertainty. They had faced numerous challenges, but their determination remained unwavering.

As they prepared for the final stages of their journey, Jamal and Keisha reflected on their achievements and the impact of their efforts. The fight for justice was nearing its end, but the dangers they faced were still very real.

They knew that their journey was far from over, and they were prepared to confront whatever challenges lay ahead. The road to justice was marked by danger and uncertainty, but Jamal and Keisha were ready to see it through to the end.

End of Chapter 27

Chapter 28: Unraveling the Web

The safe house felt more like a bunker as Jamal and Keisha continued their preparations for the impending danger. The increased threat from Hartman's associates loomed large, and their focus remained on staying one step ahead of the chaos that had engulfed the area. The fight for justice was reaching its climax, and they were determined to see it through.

Morning light filtered through the blinds, casting a soft glow on the secure hideout. Jamal and Keisha were already awake, having spent the night monitoring news updates and reviewing their plans. The room was filled with a palpable tension, a mixture of anticipation and anxiety.

Keisha was at her laptop, skimming through the latest intelligence reports. "The authorities have made some progress, but Hartman's associates are still a significant threat. There's talk of further retaliation, and the situation remains highly unpredictable."

Jamal, pacing the room, nodded in agreement. "We need to stay vigilant. If there's a possibility of further attacks, we have to be ready to act quickly."

As they discussed their strategy, Jamal's phone rang. It was Rick, his voice urgent. "Jamal, Keisha, there's been a new development. Hartman's associates are rumored to be planning a major move tonight. It could be an attempt to disrupt the investigation or target key figures."

Jamal's expression grew serious. "What kind of move?"

Rick replied, "It's unclear, but it's substantial enough to warrant concern. You need to be extra cautious and be prepared for any potential threats."

Keisha exchanged a worried glance with Jamal. "We should review our security measures again and make sure we're prepared for any scenario."

Throughout the day, Jamal and Keisha worked tirelessly to ensure their safety. They reviewed their security protocols, checked their emergency supplies, and made final adjustments to their evacuation plans. The threat of Hartman's associates made every detail critical, and they were determined not to leave anything to chance.

In the late afternoon, Karen called with an update. "The authorities have identified several potential targets for tonight's planned attack. They're increasing security around these locations, but there's still a risk of further disruption."

Jamal's face was grim. "What's the current situation with Hartman's network? Are there any new leads on their plans?"

Karen replied, "The intelligence is still coming in, but it's clear that Hartman's associates are preparing for a significant move. The authorities are working to intercept any potential threats, but you need to remain on high alert."

As evening approached, the tension in the safe house was almost unbearable. Jamal and Keisha continued to monitor the situation, keeping a close eye on the news and any developments related to Hartman's associates. The safe house had become a focal point of their struggle—a place where every sound and every shadow could signal a new threat.

In the early evening, Keisha received a call from her contact in the local law enforcement community. "Keisha, I've got some critical information. There's a credible threat targeting a highprofile location tonight. The authorities are doing everything they can to prevent it, but it's essential to stay prepared."

Keisha relayed the information to Jamal, who was already planning their next steps. "We need to be ready to move if necessary. The situation is escalating, and we can't afford to be caught off guard."

As the night fell, Jamal and Keisha prepared for the possibility of having to relocate. They packed their essentials and reviewed their evacuation plans one final time. The threat from Hartman's associates was imminent, and they knew that their next actions could be crucial.

In the midst of their preparations, Jamal took a moment to reflect on their journey. "We've been through so much to get here. This is the final stretch, and we need to stay focused."

Keisha nodded, her expression resolute. "We've made it this far, and we're not going to let anything stop us now."

As the hours ticked by, the news reports continued to update with information about the ongoing situation. The authorities were working tirelessly to manage the threat, and the media coverage was extensive. Jamal and Keisha stayed in close contact with Karen and their network, gathering any new intelligence that could impact their safety.

In the late hours of the night, Jamal received a call from Rick. "Jamal, Keisha, I've just received word that there's been a significant disruption at one of the targeted locations. The authorities are responding, but there may be further implications."

Jamal's heart raced. "What does this mean for us?"

Rick replied, "It's hard to say for sure, but it's crucial to remain vigilant. The situation is fluid, and there could be additional threats."

As the night wore on, Jamal and Keisha remained on high alert. They continued to monitor the situation and stayed prepared to act if necessary. The safe house, while providing temporary refuge, was a constant reminder of the dangers they faced.

In the early morning hours, the news reports began to reflect the aftermath of the night's events. There were reports of increased security measures and ongoing investigations, but the full extent of the situation was still unclear.

Jamal and Keisha took a moment to regroup. The threat from Hartman's associates had intensified, but their resolve remained strong. They knew that their fight for justice was nearing its climax, and they were determined to see it through.

As dawn broke, the situation was still in flux. The authorities were working to assess the damage and prevent further attacks, and the media continued to cover the unfolding events. Jamal and Keisha remained vigilant, ready to respond to any new developments.

Karen called with an update. "The situation is stabilizing, but there's still a risk of further disruption. The authorities are working to contain the threat, and there's a renewed focus on preventing additional attacks."

Jamal's face was determined. "We'll stay on high alert and continue to monitor the situation. We're prepared for any potential threats."

The day unfolded with a mixture of relief and tension. The immediate threat from Hartman's associates had been managed, but the situation remained volatile. Jamal and Keisha continued to stay on top of the news and any developments related to the ongoing investigation.

In the evening, they took a moment to reflect on their journey. The safe house had become a symbol of their struggle—a place where they had faced numerous challenges and dangers. As they prepared for the final stages of their fight, they were reminded of the significance of their efforts.

Jamal and Keisha knew that their journey was approaching its end, but the fight for justice was far from over. They remained resolute, ready to confront whatever challenges lay ahead. The road to justice was marked by uncertainty and danger, but they were prepared to see it through to the end. **End of Chapter 28**

Chapter 29: A Fractured Empire

The day after the attacks had left Union County in a state of disarray. The early morning hours were marked by a somber quiet that blanketed the once bustling streets. Jamal and Keisha had spent the previous night in a state of high alert, but as dawn approached, they found themselves grappling with the reality of their situation. Hartman's network had been severely disrupted, but the remnants of his empire still posed a threat. The battle was far from over.

Jamal and Keisha woke early, their sleep disturbed by the constant hum of uncertainty. The safe house had become a sanctuary in the midst of chaos, but the ongoing threat was a stark reminder that their fight was not yet over.

Jamal, dressed in a simple black hoodie and jeans, stared out the window at the stillness of the morning. The once vibrant neighborhood now seemed eerily quiet, a reflection of the turmoil that had shaken the community. Keisha joined him, her face pale and tired.

"We need to assess the situation," Keisha said, her voice low. "The authorities have made progress, but there's still a lot we don't know. Hartman's associates could still be planning something."

Jamal nodded, turning to face her. "Let's go over our plans again. We need to be prepared for any new developments."

As they reviewed their plans, Jamal received a message from Karen. "The situation is still unfolding.

The authorities have managed to stabilize some areas, but there are reports of continued threats. Hartman's associates are known for their unpredictability."

Jamal read the message aloud, and Keisha's expression hardened. "We need to stay sharp. If Hartman's associates are still out there, we could be at risk."

They spent the morning reviewing their evacuation routes and securing their supplies. The safe house was stocked with essentials, but the risk of needing to relocate at a moment's notice meant they had to be extra cautious.

The afternoon brought a flurry of activity. News reports continued to cover the fallout from the attacks, and the authorities were working to restore order. Jamal and Keisha stayed glued to the news, their eyes scanning for any information that might affect their safety.

In a rare moment of respite, Jamal and Keisha took a break from their preparations. They sat in the living room, their bodies aching from the constant tension. The weight of their situation was beginning to take its toll, and they found solace in each other's company. "Do you think it'll ever end?" Keisha asked, her voice tinged with weariness.

Jamal took a deep breath, his gaze fixed on the TV screen. "I don't know. We've come this far, and we've made a difference. But until Hartman's network is completely dismantled, we have to stay vigilant."

As evening approached, the atmosphere in the safe house was charged with anticipation. The reports of continued threats made it clear that Hartman's associates were still a significant danger. Jamal and Keisha were ready to respond to any new developments, their preparations meticulous and thorough.

Karen called with an update. "The authorities are making progress, but there are still concerns about potential retaliatory attacks. It's crucial to remain on high alert and be prepared for any eventuality."

Jamal's expression was resolute. "We're ready. We've gone through our plans, and we're prepared to take action if needed."

Nightfall brought with it a new layer of uncertainty. The streets outside the safe house were eerily silent, a stark contrast to the chaos of the previous days. Jamal and Keisha continued to monitor the news, their eyes scanning for any updates that might impact their safety.

In the late hours, Jamal received a call from Rick. "Jamal, Keisha, I've got some critical information. There are reports of increased activity from Hartman's associates in a nearby area. It's possible they're planning something significant."

Jamal's heart raced. "What kind of activity?"

Rick replied, "It's not entirely clear, but there's enough evidence to suggest a coordinated effort. You should be prepared for anything."

Keisha looked at Jamal, her face pale. "We need to be ready to move if necessary. The threat is still very real."

Jamal nodded, his resolve unwavering. "Let's review our evacuation plans one more time and ensure that we can act quickly if needed."

The night was marked by a sense of urgency as Jamal and Keisha made final preparations. They packed their essentials and reviewed their plans, their minds focused on the potential threats that loomed. The safe house provided temporary refuge, but the dangers outside were still very real.

As they prepared, Keisha took a moment to reflect on their journey. "We've been through so much. It's hard to believe we're still fighting this battle."

Jamal nodded, his gaze steady. "We've come a long way, but we're not done yet. We need to stay focused and see this through to the end."

In the early hours of the morning, the situation continued to evolve. The news reports were filled with updates on the ongoing investigation and the authorities' efforts to manage the threat. Jamal and Keisha remained vigilant, their eyes glued to the screen as they waited for new information.

Karen called with another update. "The authorities are intensifying their efforts to prevent further attacks. There's still a risk, but they're making progress in stabilizing the situation."

Jamal's face was set in determination. "We'll stay on high alert and continue to monitor the situation. We're prepared for any potential threats."

The day dawned with a mixture of relief and tension. The immediate threat from Hartman's associates had been managed, but the situation remained volatile. Jamal and Keisha took a moment to regroup, their thoughts focused on the final stages of their fight.

In the afternoon, Jamal and Keisha received a visit from Karen. She arrived with a stack of documents and a look of determination. "The authorities have made significant progress, but there's still work to be done. We need to stay focused and continue our efforts."

Jamal and Keisha welcomed her into the safe house, and they spent the afternoon discussing their next steps. The progress made in dismantling Hartman's network was encouraging, but the fight was far from over.

As the evening approached, Jamal and Keisha reflected on their journey. The safe house had become a symbol of their struggle—a place where they had faced numerous challenges and dangers. They knew that their fight for justice was nearing its end, but the dangers they faced were still very real.

Jamal and Keisha remained focused on their goals, determined to see their efforts through to the end. The road to justice was marked by uncertainty and danger, but they were prepared to confront whatever challenges lay ahead.

As night fell, they took a moment to rest, their minds filled with the knowledge that their fight was not yet over. The journey had been long and arduous, but they were ready to face whatever came next.

End of Chapter 29

Chapter 30: The Final Confrontation

The atmosphere in the safe house was tense as Jamal and Keisha prepared for what could be the final chapter in their fight against Hartman and his network. The authorities had made significant progress, but the remnants of Hartman's empire were still a threat. The final confrontation was drawing near, and Jamal and Keisha knew that their actions in the coming hours could determine the outcome of their struggle.

The morning began with a sense of urgency. Jamal and Keisha reviewed their plans one last time, their minds focused on the potential dangers that lay ahead. They had been through so much, but the fight was not over. The remnants of Hartman's network were still out there, and they needed to be prepared for anything.

Karen arrived at the safe house with a grim expression. "The authorities have identified a key location where Hartman's associates are believed to be gathering. It's crucial that you stay on high alert and be prepared for any potential threats."

Jamal nodded, his face determined. "We're ready. We've prepared for this moment, and we won't back down now."

Keisha's eyes were filled with resolve. "We need to ensure that we're ready to act if necessary. The final confrontation could be imminent."

As the day progressed, Jamal and Keisha received updates from Karen and their network. The authorities were closing in on Hartman's associates, but the danger remained. The location identified by the authorities was heavily guarded, and the risk of a final showdown was high.

In the late afternoon, Jamal and Keisha prepared to move. They packed their essentials and reviewed their plans once more, their minds focused on the final confrontation. The safe house had served its purpose, but it was time to take action.

Karen drove them to a discreet location near the identified target. As they approached, the tension was palpable. The authorities were already on-site, working to secure the area and prepare for any potential threats.

Jamal and Keisha met with Karen and a few trusted contacts. "The authorities have set up a perimeter around the location. They're ready for any confrontation, but the situation remains volatile."

Jamal's eyes were sharp with determination. "We'll stay in contact and be prepared to act if needed. This is the final step in our fight."

As night fell, the scene was set for the final confrontation. The authorities had secured the area, and Jamal, Keisha, and their team were on high alert. The location was a significant target, and the risk of a final showdown was high.

Jamal and Keisha waited anxiously as the authorities prepared for the operation. The tension was almost unbearable as they monitored the situation from a safe distance. The sound of police radios and the distant murmur of voices created an atmosphere of anticipation.

Karen approached them with an update. "The authorities are ready to move in. The location is heavily guarded, and there's a risk of significant confrontation. Be prepared for anything."

Jamal's expression was resolute. "We're ready. We've come this far, and we won't let anything stand in our way."

The operation began with a flurry of activity. The authorities moved in, their tactical teams prepared for any potential threats. The sound of sirens and the crackle of police radios filled the air as the final confrontation unfolded.

Jamal and Keisha watched from their vantage point, their hearts pounding with anticipation. The authorities were making progress, but the situation was still fluid. The remnants of Hartman's network were determined to resist, and the confrontation was intense.

As the night wore on, the authorities worked tirelessly to secure the area and apprehend those involved in the network. The situation was chaotic, but the final showdown was a critical step in dismantling Hartman's empire.

In the early hours of the morning, the operation was nearing its end. The authorities had managed to secure the area and apprehend several key figures from Hartman's network. The final confrontation had been intense, but the progress made was significant.

Jamal and Keisha, exhausted but relieved, met with Karen and the authorities. "The operation was successful," Karen said, her expression one of cautious optimism. "Hartman's network has been significantly disrupted, and several key figures have been apprehended."

Jamal's face reflected a mix of exhaustion and determination. "We've made it through, but the fight for justice continues. There's still work to be done."

Keisha nodded in agreement. "We've come a long way, and we need to continue our efforts to ensure that the impact of our work is lasting."

As dawn broke, Jamal and Keisha took a moment to reflect on their journey. The safe house had been a symbol of their struggle, a place where they had faced numerous challenges and dangers. The final confrontation had marked a significant turning point in their fight for justice.

Karen, Jamal, and Keisha gathered for a brief debriefing. "The authorities are continuing their work to secure the area and assess the impact of the operation," Karen said. "Your efforts have made a significant difference, and the progress made is a testament to your determination."

Jamal and Keisha exchanged a look of relief. The immediate threat had been managed, but their work was far from over. They remained committed to seeing their efforts through to the end, ensuring that the impact of their work would be felt for years to come.

As the sun rose, Jamal and Keisha began to think about their next steps. The fight for justice had reached a critical juncture, but there was still more to be done. They knew that their journey was not yet complete, and they were determined to continue their efforts.

Karen, Jamal, and Keisha shared a moment of quiet reflection. The challenges they had faced had been daunting, but their resolve had remained unwavering. The final confrontation had been a pivotal moment in their struggle, but the fight for justice was an ongoing battle.

Jamal and Keisha were ready to face whatever came next, their commitment to their cause stronger than ever. The road ahead was uncertain, but they were prepared to confront any challenges that lay ahead.

End of Chapter 30

Epilogue: The Dawn of a New Era

165

Months after the final confrontation, the impact of Jamal and Keisha's efforts was beginning to be felt across Eastwood. The authorities had made significant progress in dismantling Hartman's network, and the community was beginning to heal from the trauma of the attacks. Jamal and Keisha had become symbols of resilience and determination, their fight for justice leaving a lasting mark on the community.

The safe house, once a symbol of their struggle, had been repurposed into a community center dedicated to supporting those affected by the crisis. The center offered resources for education, job training, and counseling, helping individuals rebuild their lives and find hope in the aftermath of the chaos.

Jamal and Keisha continued their work, their efforts focused on creating a positive impact in the community. They had faced numerous challenges, but their commitment to their cause had remained unwavering. The road to justice had been long and arduous, but their journey had paved the way for a brighter future.

As they looked toward the future, Jamal and Keisha knew that their work was far from over. The fight for justice was an ongoing battle, but they were prepared to face whatever challenges lay ahead.

Their journey had been marked by struggle and triumph, and they were ready to continue their efforts to create a better world.

The dawn of a new era had begun, and Jamal and Keisha were at the forefront of a movement that sought to bring hope and change to their community. Their legacy was one of courage, resilience, and determination—a testament to the power of the human spirit in the face of adversity.

THE END

www.ingramcontent.com/pod-product-compliance
Lightning Source LLC
Chambersburg PA
CBHW071617150726

48000CB00004B/1763